The Sober Companion

Emily Ford

The Sober Companion © 2015 Emily Ford
www.emilyfordworld.com

Editing by Lizzy Ford
www.lizzyford.com

Cover photo © Tomáš Hašlar via Fotolia.com

ISBN: 1623782082
ISBN-13: 978-1623782085

Dedication

This book is dedicated to anyone that has been abused, bullied, or persecuted because of their skin color, sexual orientation, gender, religion, disability, economic status, or lifestyle choice.
Oppression is a fear-based sickness that can and must be cured.
(Emily Ford)

" …to me the earth's most explosive and pernicious evil is racism, the inability of God's creatures to live as One, especially in the Western world." (Malcolm X)

"The idea that some lives matter less is the root of all that is wrong with the world." (Dr. Paul Farmer)

"Every single American - gay, straight, bisexual, transgender – every single American deserves to be treated equally in the eyes of the law and in the eyes of our society." (President Obama)

Love
An intense feeling of deep affection

Romance
A feeling of excitement and mystery associated with love

Chapter One

"Elias Alexander?"

Eli stirs from his wandering thoughts and feigns a smile. The portly woman looks down at him through thick gold-rimmed glasses after glancing over the manila file in her hands. He hides his aversion as his enhanced sense of smell picks up her strong body odor, the result of sweating under the thick layers of her frumpy wool clothes.

Eli stands and straightens his black suit jacket. With matching black undershirt, black tie and pants, and shiny black dress shoes, he is dressed more for a funeral than a meeting with the parole officer. Given his strikingly handsome features, his cool smooth skin with a light five o'clock shadow, dark brooding eyes, and stylish black hair, he emits a sexy aura of youth and confidence. Turned into a vampire at age 29, he is the eternal image of a healthy young man in his prime.

"Follow me," she says curtly, her face showing evidence of exhaustion.

By the looks of it, the harried woman does this dozens of times a day with little time for rest. She leads him through soft carpeted hallways past office doors, some open and some closed. The entire building floor reverberating with the white noise of ringing phones and conversations. She leads him into the last office at the end of a long hallway.

"Sit here," she says. She eyeballs him while he courteously ducks around her and makes his way to the plush leather seat.

"Thank you," he says in his kindest voice. He manages another smile, but it fades quickly as he watches her stare at him without a hint of compassion. "Your parole officer will be in shortly."

She turns on her heel and hurries out of the office, pulling the thick wood door closed behind her.

Eli relaxes, relieved to see the cranky woman leave. He glances around the office admiring the 19th Century décor. The interior decorator was evidently a vampire from the era and did an immaculate job of recreating the ambiance of England in the 1800's. For a plain brick building that looks like any other in New York City, the interior of this one is timeless and familiar.

His mind wanders to the years spent with Elizabeth and he warms at her memory. Her flowing golden brown hair and beautiful face, her smooth porcelain skin and her eyes crystal blue are forefront in his mind. She always seemed to be smiling with her sensual, supple berry-colored lips.

For a millennium now, every time she dies, he usually manages to find her again. Upon reincarnation, she is always named Elizabeth, and she always looks the same. Her reincarnation was different than any he'd ever heard of, which he attributes to the witch's curse. But his heart sinks as he remembers even though he hasn't found his Elizabeth in this generation yet, they are always fated to end the same way: Elizabeth dies in her twenty fifth year of life and she never lets him turn her into a vampire so they can be together forever. It's something he has never fully understood, but attributes it to the curse as well. He remains in a torturous cycle of finding her, getting her to fall in love with him, and watching her die.

The door opens and rattles him from his pained thoughts of Elizabeth.

"Ah, Elias. Sorry I'm late." The parole officer shakes his hand as he breezes into the room and takes his seat behind the desk.

"It is no problem," Elias says, smiling at the notion that these *parole officers* wear a suit and tie and carry files and folders as opposed to guns and badges. He still finds it hard to believe the humans now have methods to mask the scent of their blood in order to prevent piquing the vampires' appetites.

"My name is David Carey, your sobriety parole officer. I am glad to have you, Elias." He flips through Elias's file. "I've read a lot about you and I must say, I am very impressed with your decision to go through with this."

"It is the best decision to be made," Elias says. "The only decision to be made."

"Yes, well a vampire as well-known as you will no doubt spur an increase in participants of the program. You will earn a lot of supporters by doing this, from both humans and vampires."

"I am here because I wish to show my respect and obedience to the law. Nothing more."

David nods. He's an observant man of great patience and takes the time to thoroughly research his clients before meeting them. "It took a lot of courage to turn State's evidence. You turned in a lot of dangerous Vampire-Americans. I'm sure that was very difficult."

Eli smiles again. "Like I said. It had to be done."

"Well, in any case, we're glad to have you. How are you enjoying life in New York City? How's your apartment working for you? You're in Greenwich Village, correct?"

"Correct. It is very nice," Eli says politely.

"And you keep your temporary Vampire Visa with you at all times?"

"Yes, of course," Eli says, hiding his amusement at the irony that vampires need a Visa in their own country to avoid arrest and persecution.

"You successfully completed blood rehab, and you're ready for the next step?"

Eli shudders at the memory of his blood rehab. It was the longest, most arduous six months of his life. Considering he has been alive for a millennium, he would prefer to be hanged, drawn, and quartered in 1351 England than go through blood rehab again. He hopes he can sustain his new diet of synthetic blood, but he isn't without concern that his thousand years of live blood feeding could make his goal hard to sustain.

"I am ready," Eli answers. "What exactly does it entail?"

"You will be assigned a sober companion who will live with you. Your sober companion will accompany you to work as well as to any social functions. Basically you will be attached at the hip for the next six months after which time your progress will be evaluated. The board will then make the determination as to whether or not you are ready for legal independence. Do you have any questions?"

"Will the sober companion be human?"

"Yes. But not to worry. He'll be medicated so you will not be able to smell his blood."

Eli exhales in relief. "Oh I am glad. I was concerned for a moment. That might have made it very difficult."

"We understand the unique needs of the sober Vampire-American," David says, his voice soft and warm. "We will do everything we can to facilitate your total rehabilitation. Also, you will attend sobriety meetings once a week with your peers. Any humans involved in leading the meetings will also be medicated, for your comfort."

"How does that work anyway? The medication – how does it mask the blood scent? I have always been curious."

David chuckles. "Modern science is remarkable these days, my friend. In essence, the medication alters human blood on a chemical level, temporarily. Humans must inject the medication daily to maintain adequate blood levels. So you may see your companion initiate injections on himself. Do not be alarmed if you do."

"Is it safe? I mean, altering the chemical nature of blood seems like it would have side effects."

"It's safe in the short-term. Sober companions are limited in the length of their assignments. A six-month assignment is followed by one month off, so their body can repair any damage that may have been done. And no sober companion is allowed more than six assignments in a lifetime."

Eli raises his eyebrows. "Sounds like a lot to go through for a human. Why do they even do this? Why do they choose to help vampires after all that has happened between us?"

David smiles warmly. "The depth of human compassion is endless, Eli. We do not wish for you to endure hardships because of your race. We want equality, and justice, for all races."

A flashback to the dark days of American slavery and segregation runs through Eli's mind. He never understood why humans used skin color as a means to determine who was superior to another. In the vampire world, age is the ultimate determination of physical strength, though there are a lot of other factors based on merit and bloodlines that either elevate or lower a vampire's station in life.

"Do you have any questions?"

David's voice pulls his mind away from thoughts of the past. "Um, just one question. You said that my sober companion will accompany me everywhere. Does he not need to sleep? Because since I do not sleep, how will they know what I am doing when he is sleeping?"

"It is physically impossible for your sober companion to guard you twenty four seven," David says. "The element of trust between you two is paramount. Sleeping helps build that trust, and prepares you for your subsequent independence after you complete the program."

"Makes sense," Eli says, impressed with the thoroughness of thought that goes into the program.

"Just remember, Elias. Your sober companion is the key to your independence. If you relapse, they will report you to the board. The consequences are steep, even for a slip up. So please take this seriously and do everything in your power to adhere to sobriety."

"Understood," Eli says.

David stands and shakes Eli's cold hand. "Good luck to you,

Elias. Expect your sober companion later this evening."

"Thank you, David."

Despite saying otherwise, Eli is full of questions about the program. The city streets and sidewalks are buzzing with the evening rush hour traffic on his walk home. He ruminates over the events of the past six months, including his decision to turn in vampires he had known for centuries to the authorities to avoid his own capital punishment. His act of vampire heresy occurred in Boston, and he was then relocated into vampire witness protection and blood rehab in New York City.

The early autumn air cools quickly as the sun sets on a horizon forever obscured by the bulky skyscrapers of the city's skyline. Just a block from his two story townhouse, a woman with long dark hair catches his eye as she passes by on the sidewalk. She's not his Elizabeth, but she reminds him of her.

Where is she? He feels the familiar desperation to find her. The last time he saw her was 1961, in Boston. He could never be certain when or where he would meet the reincarnated Elizabeth, but it has been over fifty years now. *Could he have missed her? Did something change? Is something wrong?* His soul yearns for her as it does every time he searches for her. His heart aches as he recalls the pain he feels when he watches her die. Afraid to admit to himself that he loathes the day he'll see her die again, he hides his own relief that he *hasn't* found her yet. Love is grand, but there has been nothing more painful for him, not even the blood rehab.

That evening, he allows his thoughts to linger on Elizabeth and their doomed love affair stretching a thousand years. Inside the Victorian style townhouse, he sits motionless in his favorite leather recliner, lost in his mind.

A firm knock at the front door rouses him and he shakes his head to symbolically shake her from his mind's eye. The hardwood floors groan beneath his shoes as he strides to the entryway, the familiar sound one that transcends centuries of fine living.

Eli opens the door and feels the wind supernaturally drawn from his lungs. It is something that only happens when he meets the reincarnated Elizabeth anew each time: the shock, the familiarity and excitement, the longing, and the desperation all overtaking his senses.

Chapter Two

"Elias Alexander?"

"You're not Elizabeth!" Eli blurts out.

Before him stands a young man, mid-twenties, with light brown hair and blue eyes. He is dressed in jeans and a black wool coat with scarf, holding a single piece of luggage akin to that of an overnight bag. He's handsome but his face is taught and his eyes glare with some degree of heat.

"Are you Elias Alexander?" The young man repeats, visibly annoyed.

Eli shakes his head and blinks rapidly. *What the hell just happened?*

"I'm sorry. Yes, I am," he stammers.

"My name is Eric Wayne. I've been assigned to be your sober companion."

Eli tilts his head, still trying to figure out why the sight of this young man just knocked the wind out of him. He can't smell his blood, so it has nothing to do with hunger. *But he looks like her.*

"Didn't David Carey tell you to expect me?"

Eli lightly smacks his forehead with his palm. "Yes, yes he did. I apologize. My mind was somewhere else." He smiles at his guest and searches the strangely familiar blue eyes for an answer.

"Are you going to let me in, or is there going to be a problem?"

The hostility in Eric's voice seems forced, but Eli doesn't wish to further upset his sober companion. His entire future rides on pleasing this guy, and he does not intend to screw up his one shot at becoming a legally independent Vampire-American.

"Yes, of course! Come in." He holds the door open wide as Eric enters and locks it behind them. "Shall I show you around?"

"Did you think we were going to play Monopoly or something?" Eric stares coldly at him.

Eli is taken aback by the rude comment. "Uh, no."

"Let's get one thing straight, right now," Eric says, stepping close to Eli.

Despite being in close proximity to the legendarily ruthless and violent vampire, Eric doesn't feel afraid and quietly seethes inside. Falling short of the vampire by several inches in height, he nonetheless puffs his chest and plants his feet in a wide stance as he glares into the monster's dark eyes.

"We are not friends. I'm here to make sure you don't screw up, that's it. If you so much as sneeze at a drop of live human blood, your ass will go back to rehab. Anything more than that and you'll be put to death. Those are the terms you agreed to, and those are the terms that I will enforce. I go where you go. I'm in your face every second of every day except when I'm sleeping. You will go to any meeting I tell you to. Cross me and this arrangement, and your freedom is terminated. Are we clear?"

Eli suppresses a chuckle while he digests the information. This short, angry kid is threatening his life but he can't help feeling like bursting into laughter. There is nothing intimidating about Eric. It is obvious to Eli that Eric has a gentle spirit, but something is agitating him. Not to mention the fact that Eric makes him feel like he just came home again, the same way he feels when finding Elizabeth.

Eli holds up his hands in faux surrender. "Clear!" he says. He is unable to stop the wide smile from spreading across his lips.

"Is something funny?" Eric says, the smile provoking his anger even more.

Eli chuckles. "No! It's just … David said something about the reason you humans do this work is because you feel compassionate towards vampires, but I don't get that from you."

"I'm not here because I'm compassionate," Eric says. He looks down as a dark thought passes through his mind.

"Oh, and we don't … sneeze," Eli says.

"Excuse me?"

"Vampires, uh we don't … sneeze." Eli is pleased by his own joke but cringes when he realizes Eric is not.

An awkward moment of silence passes and Eli helps ease the tension by stepping back.

"Okay, now that we have that straightened out, how about I give you that tour?"

"Fine," Eric says.

Eli leads the salty companion through the townhouse and ends by showing Eric to his room directly across the hall from his own. Eric tosses his bag onto the bed.

"Is your refrigerator stocked with synthetic blood?"

"Yep, filled to the brim," Eli says casually. "Good to go on the synthetic. Love that stuff."

Eric narrows his eyes. "What is your feeding schedule?"

"Same as in rehab. Every eight hours."

Eric nods, pleased. "Good. Come with me into the bathroom. I need to take a sample."

"A sample?"

"You thought we would just be hanging out talking? Yes, a sample. How else will I be able to confirm that you're clean?"

Eli fights the urge to roll his eyes. "Yes, of course. My mistake," he says. He mumbles under his breath as he turns.

"What did you say?" Eric says behind him.

"Nothing! I mumble sometimes. It's just a thing I do," Eli says, shooting a fake smile over his shoulder.

"Huh."

"Huh – what?" Eli enters the bathroom and turns around to face Eric.

"Nothing, it's just that you have a reputation for being a bad ass. I don't see it."

Eli is beginning to wonder if he will be able to handle having such a disagreeable sober companion around him all the time, and if his choice of sobriety is even worth the pain and inconvenience.

"Okay, so what do you need from me?"

Eric opens the kit he retrieved from his bag and pulls out a long cotton swab.

"Open your mouth," he orders.

Eli complies and allows Eric to roll a dry cotton swab on the inside of his mouth. He watches as Eric rubs it on a test strip and waits for it to turn colors. The strip turns blue, indicating no consumption of live human blood within the past 24 hours.

"You pass test number one," Eric says. He tosses the strip in the small trash can on the bathroom floor and closes up the kit.

"I knew I would," Eli jokes, trying to lighten the companion's mood. Eric looks up from the kit and glares at him. "You know, because I've been clean for six months, so ..."

Eric nods. "Good. Make sure it stays that way."

He retreats from the bathroom and walks into his bedroom, stowing the test kit away in the nightstand next to the bed. Eli trails him so closely that Eric turns around and jumps, startled to see the vampire right on his heels.

"Sorry," Eli says, hands flying up again as he sees Eric's posture go rigid. He steps back to give the grumpy guest more room.

"Is something wrong?" Eric asks, his voice tinged with both anger and anxiety.

"No, it's just that you seem really familiar. Have we met before?"

Eric shakes his head. "I would remember meeting someone like *you*."

Offended, Eli raises his eyebrows. "Someone like me? What's that supposed to mean?"

"It means," Eric begins as he walks around to the other side of the bed pulling his bag with him as he goes, "you're basically a legend. I don't get many clients as old as you. Or as ..." He silences abruptly, now unzipping his bag to unpack it.

"As what?"

"Dangerous."

Eli chuckles. "Are you worried about being here?" He walks around the bed, watching Eric pull out perfectly folded clothes and placing them on the mattress. "Look. I'm not going to hurt you, Eric. It's me who should be afraid of *you*. My freedom lies in *your* hands."

"I'm not afraid of you," Eric says flatly.

"Okay. Good," Eli says.

He continues to watch as Eric pulls out a surprising quantity of clothing from the small bag. He has everything folded and packed so economically that it reminds Eli of watching an inconceivable amount of clowns spill out of a miniature clown car. Elizabeth was always a stickler for neatness and order too. He realizes the correct term for it now days is Obsessive Compulsive Disorder.

"Uh, so, are you a bit OCD?" Eli says with a laugh.

Eric glances at him sideways but continues with his task. "Why do you say that?"

Eli points to the perfectly folded and now lined up clothes. "Just an observation."

Eric clears his throat. "David didn't tell me about your occupation. What do you do?"

Eli plops down on the bed, too energetically for Eric's comfort because a pile of shirts topples over as he does. He observes Eric's silent death glare and scoots farther away so as not to further disrupt the important task in progress.

Annoyed by the vampire's reckless disregard of the order of his clothing piles and subsequent lengthy silence, Eric straightens and stares him down. "Well? What, are you a used car salesman or something?"

Eli laughs. "No, I'm not a used car salesman. Although, I tried that once, and pretty much hated every second of it. I really don't like sales, you know? If it's not something I don't believe in, I don't want to waste my energy trying to convince someone to buy something they don't need anyway."

"So what do you do then, Elias?" Eric takes the first pile of shirts to the adjacent dresser and finds the proper drawer for them.

"I work with the police homicide department."

Eric whips his head around. "Seriously?"

"Yep."

"How is that even possible? I didn't think vampires are allowed in law enforcement, let alone in homicide?"

"It's part of my arrangement."

"How can you work for the police when you're basically in witness protection yourself?"

"The vampires I turned in were out of Boston. There shouldn't be much of a threat to me here, especially given the size of the city's population."

"But it's still risky, right? Don't they say members of law enforcement live a high profile life since they deal with the bad guys all day? Someone could make your identity and rat you out."

"It's a risk the board is willing to take," Eli says, looking down at the hardwood floor. "And I don't really care if they find me again. It's all a lost cause anyway."

"What is?"

Eli's thoughts drift to Elizabeth. The heartache of losing her over and over again never goes away. He had hoped it would get better, become easier to endure, but that is never the case.

"Elias?"

Eric's question interrupts Eli's trip down memory lane. "Hmm?"

"You said it's all a lost cause. What is?"

"Nothing. Um, call me Eli. Please." The cell phone in his

pocket rings. He stands and takes out the phone to answer it. "Hello, Captain," he says. "All right. Text me the address, I'll be there soon." Just as he hangs up from the call, an alarm goes off on the phone. He looks at the screen. "Ah, dinner time," he says, flashing it at Eric.

"Was that a work call?" Eric asks.

"Yep. You're in luck, you get to see your first crime scene on your first day!"

Eric's eyes drop as a memory flashes through his mind. "It's not my first crime scene," he mumbles.

Just then, Eric's watch begins to beep, a reminder that it's time for his injection. "We seem to be on the same schedule," he says. "You eat and I'll take my injection. Meet you downstairs."

Eli lingers to watch as Eric withdraws a pack of syringes and two vials of a clear liquid. "Is that the stuff?"

Eric holds it up for him to see. "That's the stuff."

"So that's what keeps you from smelling like dinner, eh?" Eli's attempt at humor is met with Eric's cold stare. "Just kidding," he says, hiding a grimace. "Okay, I'll be downstairs when you're ready. And dress warm because we may be outside for a bit tonight."

Eric watches Eli leave his room and listens as he jogs down the wooden steps, disappointed to discover the vampire is actually a nice guy. He seems considerate, funny, and practically warm. It makes hating him that much harder. Not to mention the odd familiarity about him that made him feel at ease as soon as he saw him. It will be a true challenge to keep being a hard ass to this vampire.

Eric takes the pack of syringes and vials to the bathroom and takes a needle out of its sterile packaging. He plunges it through the rubber seal of one vial and withdraws it after sucking up the appropriate dose. After squirting out the air bubbles through the needle tip and tapping it, he sets it down on the sink to swab the injection site with alcohol. He taps the vein, his arm already scarred from years of repeated injections. When enough of the blue vein appears, he slowly injects the clear fluid into his arm. The chemical compound produces an immediate flushing side effect and he feels the heat travel all through his body.

Here comes the pain. The heat in his veins morphs into excruciating pain he feels in every cell of his body. The syringe tumbles into the sink and his body wrenches in agony. He fiercely grits his teeth to prevent a scream from escaping his throat. He likens the experience to having his whole body catch fire and burn incessantly. He writhes while riding out the swelling waves of hellish torture. The sensation doesn't last very long, which is the only relief whenever he shoots up.

Within a minute, the pain and the heat subside. His heart rate and blood pressure return from the brink of stroke to normal. He can't hide the profuse sweating and his pale skin gleams with it, and his eyes stay bloodshot for at least a half hour afterwards. Otherwise, to the untrained eye, he is back to normal.

He gives himself another minute to regain his composure. As he stares into the mirror at his bloodshot eyes, he silently curses himself for letting it get this bad.

"Hey, are you coming?" Eli calls from the bottom of the stairs.

"Yeah," Eric answers. He hurriedly packs the injection supplies into the medicine cabinet above the sink. The fact that the medicine no longer needs to be refrigerated has further enabled his abuse of it.

Eli stands at the entryway by the front door and watches a bundled-up Eric hurry down the stairs. He immediately notices the swollen red veins in Eric's eyes, and smells the fresh batch of chemicals circulating in his veins.

"You all right?"

Eric meets his gaze only briefly, hoping to hide evidence of his addiction. "Yeah, fine," he says. "So where are we off to?"

"Midtown. There's a body in an alley," Eli says. He checks his phone for the address of the crime scene.

Three trains and twenty minutes later, Eli and Eric arrive at the scene of a fresh homicide. Red and blue police lights dance on buildings and reflect off store windows as the parked police cars block the entrance to the dark narrow alley. Two officers string yellow police tape across the entrance to contain the scene.

"Captain Meyers," Eli says as he approaches the tall lanky police veteran.

"Elias," Captain Meyers says coldly. "You know I prefer not to see your face. Unfortunately circumstances call for it tonight."

Eric is taken aback by the Captain's rudeness towards the vampire.

"This is Eric," Eli says, sweeping a hand towards him. "He is my -"

"Parole officer?" Captain Meyers interrupts.

"Sober companion," Eric corrects him.

Eli cringes at the sound of it, but knows what's coming next.

"Oh, yeah. They told me about this," Captain Meyers says, crossing his arms over his chest. He glares down at Eric. "You're responsible for making sure this deadbeat doesn't slip up and drink live blood."

Eric's eyebrows furrow. "Basically," he mutters.

"Now you listen to me," the Captain says, stepping in and shoving his face into Eric's. "You better do your damn job and make sure nothing happens, or so help me God I will throw both of your asses in jail myself. You got that?"

Eric stiffens and clears his throat. "Yes. Yes, Sir," he says.

The Captain glares at him and scans his eyes. "You high or something? Why are your eyes glassy?"

"It's the blood medication," Eric stammers. "I just took a dose and sometimes it makes my eyes look ... glassy."

"Humph. No one else mentions having that problem," the Captain says, intensifying his glare.

"Captain, we found something," an officer calls from the dumpster in the alley.

"Yeah, coming," Captain Meyers yells. He stops his interrogation of Eric and walks to the officer.

"Uh, don't mind him," Eli says with a chuckle. "He's always kind of a -"

"A dick?"

Eli laughs. "He's a good man and he does his job very well." He holds up the police tape for Eric to duck under it.

"I thought he was going to arrest me for a minute," Eric says, breathing a sigh of relief.

"I think that every time I see him," Eli says with a smile. He hands Eric a pair of latex gloves. "Crime scene," he says in response to Eric's inquisitive look.

Eric lingers back while Eli examines the crime scene. The body of a man wearing white chef's clothes lies face down in the middle of the alley. A significant pool of blood beneath his head is of great concern to Eric. Eli stoops down next to the body.

"Uh, hey," he says, stepping towards Eli and the body. He hushes his voice so the police officers won't hear him. "Isn't that blood going to bother you?"

Eli looks at the pool of blood and shakes his head. "It's dead blood. Cold. It still has some scent to it but nothing that would threaten my sobriety." He looks up and smiles at Eric's grave expression. "Relax. I'm fine with this."

Eric forces himself to stop holding his breath. Seeing a dead man's body is difficult enough, but anticipating a potentially public relapse if Eli can't handle being around the blood compounds his anxiety.

"So what exactly are you looking for?"

With gloved hands, Eli carefully touches the body and examines the clothing and contents of the pockets. "Approximate time of death, cause of death. I check for rigor mortis and examine the wounds." After his examination of the body, Eli removes one of his gloves and dips a finger into the pool of cold blood. He taps it onto the tip of his tongue.

"What the hell are you doing?" Eric hisses. "You didn't seriously just do that!"

Eli stands up. "Don't worry. This is dead blood. It is part of my examination process." He pulls out a tissue from his pocket and wipes the blood off his finger.

Eric glances around wildly to see if the police officers noticed Eli's exploit. He steps in close to whisper. "You have two seconds to explain yourself before I let Captain Caveman over there take you in!"

Eli smiles. "You don't know about residuals?"

Eric suppresses a full blown panic. He notices a condemning glance from Captain Meyers and fakes a large, toothy smile. "Residuals? I thought that was some stupid rumor! Enlighten me, and do it fast!"

"Blood isn't just a physical component to living things. It also contains a spiritual imprint of sorts, unique to each individual."

"Yeah? And?" Eric says through gritted teeth.

"When a vampire ingests human blood, we get a glimpse into the person's memories and we absorb their emotions. The older a vampire is, the closer to the original vampire bloodline, the stronger our ability is."

"This is unbelievable," Eric mutters. "Why didn't they tell me this? You'd think someone would find it a priority to tell me that you would be sampling dead people's blood to find out who murdered them!"

"Essentially, yes! That's a big part of what I do."

"Does the Captain know this?"

Eli glances at the Captain now approaching them. "He knows. But he doesn't like it one bit." Eli steps around the panicked Eric and explains the details of the murder to the Captain.

Eric is blown away by the insight Eli provides to the Captain.

The Captain grunts after Eli explains what happened and scribbles on his notepad. "So it's another lover's quarrel. We're looking for this man's ex-wife, who has allegedly arranged to have this poor schmuck ganked." He turns to an officer and repeats the information, and turns back to Eli. "We'll be in touch," he says. He walks away without another word, leaving Eric dumfounded and Eli feeling unappreciated, once again.

"That's a wrap," Eli says, removing the other glove from his hand.

"That's it?" Eric shakes his head in disbelief. "Are you sure? I mean, are you ever wrong? Are the residuals ever wrong?"

"Rarely," Eli answers. "You know your mouth is kind of hanging open," Eli says with a grin.

"Uh, wow," he says. Struggling to comprehend the gravity of the situation, he inadvertently stands stupefied and unmoving until Eli yells for him, already having crossed back under the yellow police tape.

"Eric?"

Eric snaps out of his stupor and jogs towards Eli, slowing to a respectable walk upon receiving a murderous glare from Captain Meyers. "Captain," he says politely, nodding properly. He hurries away from the crime scene and ducks under the yellow tape as Eli holds it up for him.

"That was incredible," he breathes. He glances over his shoulder to be sure they are out of earshot of the police. "I mean, you just solved a murder in, like, three seconds! Why don't all police departments use you guys for this? There wouldn't be any more cold cases, or unsolved mysteries! I mean, wow!" He hops in excitement. "This could change the entire world! Crime would plummet because everyone would be afraid to do anything for fear of getting caught right away!"

Eli's expression is somber, a contrast to Eric's excitement and optimism.

"What is your problem?" Eric says, nudging Eli with his elbow. "That was amazing! You're practically a superhero! You just solved a murder. Aren't you happy about it?"

Eli smiles warmly. "I admire your optimism, Eric. But things aren't that simple."

"What do you mean?"

"For one, there aren't many vampires my age or older that are willing to use their ability for human purposes. Most of them prefer to stay hidden anyway. And second, humans aren't ready to relinquish any degree of power or responsibility to vampires. There would be another Human-Vampire War if the public found out even a small number of crimes are being solved by vampires. We are still an abomination to most people. And, rightly so, in many cases."

"Rightly so? You don't believe you deserve a chance at equality?"

Eli glances at him. "You know, you are a bit of a contradiction," he says.

Eric stops walking and steps towards a storefront to avoid impeding the pedestrian traffic on the sidewalk. Eli stops ahead of him and turns, walking slowly back to him.

"Why am I a contradiction?"

"Well, an hour ago you seemed like you could not care less about vampires. Specifically, about me and my life. But now you call me a superhero and suggest I deserve equality? Ergo, you are contradicting yourself."

Eric knows Eli's point is valid. Since the incident, he has been extremely conflicted on the issue of vampire rights. He thought he did the right thing, but it ended up biting him in the ass. His disdain for vampires is truly just disdain for a single vampire, the one involved in the incident, but he plans to take that secret to the grave with him.

"Well?" Eli prods. "Is there an epic response in that head of yours?" Eric's inner conflict is practically palpable, but he falls silent. "Okay. We will leave it at that for now," Eli says, offering him a reprieve. "I am sure you are very tired. If we hurry we can catch the next train home."

Chapter Three

Eric walks silently beside Eli as they cross the final street to their block. His planned approach to this assignment is to maintain a comfortable distance from his client, and to critique him and judge him according to ironclad rules. But Eli already feels more like an old friend to him than a hardened vampire criminal grasping at his last chance to win legal independence. He behaves like anything but the hardened deadbeat Captain Meyers assumes he is. Eric feels his inner resolve to catch the monster in a relapse waning fast.

Deep in thought, Eric doesn't notice Eli stop cold in his tracks and let out a barely audible growl. Before he can move, a vampire launches with inhuman speed from the shadows of a short alley between apartment buildings and hauls Eli back into the shadows.

The attacking vampire throws him against the side of the brick building. Eli retaliates and strikes the vampire, his movements faster than the human eye can accurately track. The vampire punches back, and the two wrestle on their feet, slamming each other into the walls and unleashing rapid fire punches.

"Hey! Stop right now! I'm calling the cops!" Eric yells, vividly aware of the imminent danger and strangely concerned for his client's wellbeing. He watches helplessly as the attacking vampire overpowers Eli and pins him against the wall.

"Hello, Eli," the vampire purrs.

"What do you want, Jeremiah?" Eli growls.

"You know this guy? Eli, do you need help?" Eric calls, inching towards them but maintaining a safe distance.

Eli holds up a hand indicating for Eric to stay back.

"You made a lot of enemies by what you did, Elias," the vampire says. "They're looking for you."

"I wouldn't expect less," Eli says.

The vampire jerks him by the collar and shoves him hard into the wall.

"Eli!" Eric calls.

"It's okay, Eric," Eli answers, keeping his eyes on Jeremiah. "You can be put to death just being this close to me, Jeremiah. Better make this quick."

"I'm not here to kill you, Eli. I'm here to let you know that we know where you are. We're coming for you. And anyone that gets in the way," he says, turning his head to look at Eric, "will go down with you."

"That's it?" Eli laughs. He spits the blood in his mouth onto the pavement. "You came here to intimidate me? Do you really think that's wise, Jeremiah?"

"You're on synthetic, Eli. You're weak as a kitten," Jeremiah says with a maniacal laugh. "I could kill you now, but what's the fun in that? I'm looking forward to judgment day. It'll be soon, Eli. Not only will we take back power over the humans, but we'll take your head in the process."

Eric's heart drops into his stomach at the vampire's revelation. The rumors are true. The vampires are planning another war.

Eli gives Jeremiah a bloody smile. "Good luck with that," he mocks.

Jeremiah releases him and steps back, sneering. "Enjoy your

last months of existence, Elias. It will all be over for you soon." He strides towards Eric, brushing shoulders with him as he passes. He sniffs hard and grunts. "Kiss your chemical camouflage goodbye, little boy," he says. "Pretty soon you won't have your precious drugs to pacify our appetites."

Jeremiah rants and raves like a loud drunkard as he saunters off down the sidewalk, his eerie voice echoing off the brick buildings.

Eric watches Jeremiah to make sure he is actually leaving, and sighs in relief. Eli approaches him, wiping blood from his nose.

"Damn it, sometimes I really hate vampires," Eric blurts. He cringes as soon as the words come out of his mouth. He glances at Eli, who appears unfazed by his comment. "Sorry. Um, are you all right?"

"Yeah," Eli says. He hides his disappointment in Eric's comment. "Let's get inside."

The townhouse is just a short walk away.

"Wow, that guy must have been a really old vampire? He kind of beat the crap out of you," Eric says.

"He's only a couple hundred years old," Eli answers.

Eric looks at him. "Seriously? But, if you're older than him, how is it he was able to beat you?"

"It's the synthetic blood," Eli says. "It keeps us alive but that's about all. It significantly reduces our physical strength. It is all part of the human construct to keep us subdued so we don't hurt anyone."

"I know it weakens you, but I didn't realize how much. That kind of sucks for you, right?"

Eli laughs. "Would you want a bunch of primitive T-Rexes roaming the streets at full capacity? No. For humans, the primary goal in life is to survive by keeping monsters at bay. And to stay at the top of the food chain. It's instinctual."

They reach the steps to the townhouse.

"What about your primary goal in life?" Eric pauses at the bottom step. "What makes you keep going in a world that wants to keep you oppressed?"

The answer is plain and simple for Eli. Perhaps too simple for a monster like him. "It's getting late," he says, breezing up the stairs. "You should get some rest."

Around three in the morning, Eli's curiosity about his sober companion gets the better of him. After pacing in the hallway, he walks to Eric's bedroom door and pauses outside of it, listening to make sure he is asleep. When he is certain, he quietly opens the door and stands just inside the room, watching the human breathe deeply as he slumbers.

Eric's resemblance to Elizabeth is uncanny. He could easily pass as her twin brother. And the rush of emotion he experienced when opening the door for him earlier that day was indistinguishable to the way he feels each time he finds Elizabeth again.

He slips into one of his favorite memories of her from the 1800's.

They sneak away from her English home and wander into the woods. She wears a dark pink dress and the necklace he gives her each lifetime, a round white opal fitted inside gold plating hanging from a gold chain. The spring air is cool and moist, but the sunshine warms their skin and their passion for each other heats their bodies.

Elizabeth playfully runs from him, weaving behind trees and flashing him her brilliant come-hither smile as she always does. The clean breeze lifts her long hair from her shoulders and it flows around her like a ribbon.

"You are getting slow, my love," Elizabeth teases him, ducking behind a large tree trunk. She pauses, listening for the cracking of leaves and branches beneath his feet. The forest is silent save for the chirping of birds.

"I've got you!" He declares, appearing in front of her seemingly out of nowhere. He grabs her by the waist and pulls her to him.

"You cheated!" She says, laughing.

"Vampire," he says matter-of-factly.

He playfully teases her, leaning in for a kiss but pulling away at the last moment.

"Stop your teasing, Sir!" She says firmly. "A lady will not wait forever!"

"Yes, my love," he says softly, pulling her into a long, warm kiss. He pulls away and cups her cheeks with his hands. "Stay with me, Elizabeth. Forever."

Elizabeth's smile fades.

"Please! I love you so much. I want nothing else in this life but you." He senses the elation drain from her soul. "Elizabeth, why won't you let me turn you? Don't you want us to be together forever? We can be! It is right at our fingertips!"

Elizabeth sighs and shakes her head. "I cannot, my love. I do not wish to be immortal if it means having to drink blood to stay alive. It seems like a nightmare." She gently caresses his face. "Your curse hurts me like nothing else. I wish I could end it for you, I know how you suffer."

Eli lays his hands over hers, then brings them down between them. "It is not as bad as you may think, my love. You would get used to it. It wouldn't be as much of a nightmare as you fear."

He aches inside, as he knows his words are a lie. Being a slave to blood truly is a curse without end. And always having to move and change identities to avoid scrutiny from humans and their persecution is exhausting. He yearns to have Elizabeth by his side through it all, but he loves her too much to force it upon her. It must be her choice, or he would not be able to live with himself.

"Your twenty fifth birthday approaches, my love," he says grimly. "I told you how your life will end in your twenty fifth year, unless you let me change you."

Elizabeth's gaze falls to the earth.

Eli lifts her chin with his finger and plants a kiss on her soft lips. "I will never force it upon you, Elizabeth. But I need you to know that you don't have to die. You can stay with me, forever."

"There is nothing I want more, Elias," she says with a small smile. "But not like this. Not as a ..."

"Monster," he finishes her sentence. "I am sorry you are loved by a monster. If I could change this," he says, waving a hand over his face, "I would."

"You would, if you could, my love. I know this." A tear rolls down her cheek and she swipes it away before he can. "Come! We have much to explore *today while Father and Mother are away!"*

He smiles, always appreciative of her ability to remain positive in a dark world filled with anguish and oppression.

Eric stirs from his sleep long enough to roll over on his side, facing away from the door. His movement startles Eli, but he soon realizes that his intrusion goes unnoticed. In the moonlight, the only source of ambient lighting, Eli spots a familiar mark on Eric's bicep. He is sleeping in a sleeveless tank top that exposes his arm and the top of his shoulder. If Eli's heart were still beating, it would stop cold.

He slowly approaches the sleeping sober companion, pausing when the floor creaks beneath his footsteps. He holds his breath and maintains a dead quiet as he leans over the bed to peer at Eric's arm.

The mark is three inches in diameter. Despite the low light, it is brownish in color, and raised like a burn. It is the mark of the witch, the same one Elizabeth was branded with the night the curse was initiated. Eli's mouth drops open and he struggles to maintain his composure to avoid waking Eric.

The night of the curse, over a thousand years ago, floods freshly into his mind. The woman Moriah, to whom he was arranged to marry but never loved, caught him sneaking off with Elizabeth, whom he had been in love with since they were very young. No one knew Moriah was a witch, and a powerful one at that. In a jealous rage, she unleashed hell upon them.

With the help of three male vampires, the scorned woman placed eternal curses upon both her betrothed and his lover. She cursed Eli to roam the earth for eternity as an undead slave to blood, ordering one of the vampires to turn him. She cursed Elizabeth to continuously reincarnate and die in her twenty fifth year of life. She would have no memory of her past lives, and if Eli wanted her in his life he would be forced to search the earth for her and attempt to woo her into loving him again, only to watch her die a young woman. Part of Elizabeth's curse was to be born in each life with the witch's mark, which she permanently branded onto her shoulder.

Eli is overwhelmed by the memory and cold tears fall from his eyes. He covers his mouth to keep himself from crying out. Eric bears the witch's mark, but how? Is Elizabeth's soul inside him? Did he run out of time to convince Elizabeth to let him change her, and now she will never again reincarnate? Is his love lost forever?

Eli flees from the room and runs downstairs and outside, desperate for a shot of cold, fresh air. The only reason he has continued living for all these years was to look for Elizabeth. Each time he tried his best to convince her to stay with him forever, but each time she refused. Is it over now? Dread fills him. Has he missed his chance? His reason for living could be lost.

The next morning, Eric awakens to a harsh beam of sunlight shining directly in his face. He grumbles and rolls onto his back, swinging his arm over his eyes as he does. He catches a whiff of food, and his stomach growls with hunger.

"Do you always sleep in this late?"

Eli's voice from the doorway startles him. Eric jumps and sits half way up in bed. For a moment, he had forgotten that he was on another assignment and staying with a new client. He glances at his watch and groans.

"Oh, damn it! We have a meeting in an hour. I can't believe I overslept."

"Meeting?"

Eric throws back the covers on his bed and swings his legs over the side. "A sobriety meeting. Remember? The whole point of me being here is to enforce your sobriety?"

"Of course," Eli says. He points over his shoulder. "I made breakfast." Eric throws him a funny look. "I mean, if you're into that kind of thing."

"You mean eating?"

"Yeah! Eating! Hey, well that wasn't awkward at all."

Eric's eyes narrow. "Are you all right? You didn't relapse

while I was asleep, did you?"

Eli throws up his hands. "No! Of course not!"

Eric stands up and points sternly to the bathroom across the hall. "Let's go. Now," he orders.

"What? Oh, you're kidding me, right? Another test?"

"Do I look like I'm kidding? Go, now." Eric grabs the test kit from his nightstand and herds the vampire into the bathroom. He pulls out a long cotton swab and stabs it into Eli's mouth.

"Easy!" Eli slurs over the dry cotton utensil scraping his mouth.

Eric withdraws it and applies it to a test strip. "Huh, it's clean."

"You say that like you're surprised. Where's the trust, man? I even made you breakfast!"

"No, it's just, you ingested that drop of blood last night, and it doesn't register on this."

"I told you," Eli says, patting him on the shoulder as he passes. "It was dead blood."

"Interesting," Eric murmurs.

"Come on, your food is getting cold," Eli calls from the stairs.

Downstairs, Eric sits down in one of the four chairs of the small rectangular kitchen table. Before him is a mouthwatering spread of scrambled eggs, toast, sliced fruit, and coffee.

"What is this?" Eric exclaims.

Alarmed, Eli hurries to the table and examines the breakfast. "What is wrong? Is it undercooked? Overcooked? You do not like it?"

"Like it? I haven't had a home cooked breakfast like this in years!"

Eli relaxes. "Oh. Well, you're welcome," he says. He pulls out the chair opposite Eric and sits down.

Eric digs in to the breakfast. The warm eggs and crispy toast immediately satisfying his appetite. "Oh man, this is good," he says with a mouth full of eggs.

Eli chuckles. "I'm glad you like it. I'm a little surprised at how *much* you like it, though."

"Shut up. It's good," Eric says. He takes another bite and moans in satisfaction.

"So, where is the meeting?"

"It's on the west side. It shouldn't take more than twenty minutes to get there."

"Fine," Eli says, his voice tight.

Eric studies the vampire's stoic face while he wolfs down the breakfast. "You know you can't bribe me to get out of this, right?"

Eli tilts his head. "Bribe you?"

Eric nods pointedly, glancing down at his food.

Eli laughs. "You think by my making you breakfast, that I mean to bribe you?"

"The thought crossed my mind," Eric says, shoving another forkful into his mouth. "You'd be surprised what some of my clients have done to try to eek their way out of sobriety meetings."

"I do not doubt that." Eric raises his eyebrows and waits for a better answer. "I am not trying to bribe you, Eric! I just like to cook for people. It makes me feel ... normal, in a way."

"Normal, huh?"

"Yeah! Normal! Is that so hard to believe?"

Eric knows the vampire is sincere, but he is not one to let vampires off the hook easily. Not anymore. He scarfs the rest of the breakfast and swallows down the coffee.

"All right then," he says. He stands from the table and picks up his plate and utensils, bussing them to the sink. "We need to leave ... but first I have to wash these."

"You don't have to clean up," Eli says.

"No, no, it's only fair," Eric says, already rolling up his sleeves and running hot water. "Besides, I am very particular about how things get cleaned."

"Yeah, I know," Eli says, smiling wide at how Elizabeth used to double and triple clean the items in her houses.

Eric pauses, soapy hands floating above the sink as he stares at Eli's now warm and fuzzy expression.

"Is it that obvious?" Eric asks.

Eli pulls himself from his flashback of Elizabeth. "What?"

"You agreed with me about being particular about things. Do I come across as obsessive or something?"

"Oh. Uh, no! Not at all."

Eric glares at him.

"Okay, just a little, but everyone has their thing, right?"

Eric continues his mission to destroy every germ on the dishes by vigorously scrubbing them.

"Hey, can I ask you something?"

"Shoot," Eric says.

"Last night you said you hate vampires. It is totally understandable. Don't get me wrong. Many humans do. But I was just wondering if there is a specific reason?"

Eric's scrubbing slows and he looks up from the bubbly sink. He considers the question and carefully chooses his response. "I am not at liberty to discuss that with you, Elias," he says finally.

Intrigued by the mystery, Eli decides to let the issue go for now. "Fair enough," he says.

"We should get going if we want to make the meeting on time."

Chapter Four

"So what did that vampire want with you last night?" Eric asks, huffing after trying to keep up with Eli as he bounds effortlessly up the subway stairs.

Eli glances at him. "Jeremiah?"

"Yeah."

"Oh, the usual. There is another vampire war coming, etcetera, etcetera."

Eric laughs. "Etcetera? Seriously? How can you just brush something like that off? Is an impending plan for another Human-Vampire War nothing to worry about?"

"It is nothing new. Various sects of vampires have always wanted to overrun the humans and take over the world. They will never make it happen. You remember the race wars in America, right? How at first, it started as white people versus black people, but then the existence of vampires came to light and it morphed into a human versus vampire thing?"

"Yes, which explains why right now, you're a vampire and you're going to a court-ordered sobriety meeting."

"Yes. It will never be an epic takeover like those vampires want. They have delusions of grandeur. They're always plotting something, but humans and human sympathizers historically come out on top."

Just meters ahead of them on the sidewalk, a fight between two college kids has just ended, and the witnesses that linger are tending to one of the boys whose nose is pouring blood onto the pavement.

The aroma of fresh, warm blood hits Eli's nose before Eric even sees the spill. Eli's pace slows and Eric is steps ahead of him before he realizes what is happening.

After seeing the potentially lethal trigger, Eric's heart pounds and he knows he must act quickly before the blatant display of blood sets Eli off.

"Eli?" He watches Eli's face subtly twitch. The smell obviously bothers him. "Hey, let's cross the street, okay?"

The metallic perfume accosts Eli's senses and threatens to provoke the beast inside him that craves blood non-stop. He recalls the torturous pain he endured during blood rehab, and what he wouldn't do to avoid going through that again. Vampires call it the Dry Death, when for whatever reason their supply of live blood gets cut off. He is grateful when Eric steps in front of him, blocking his view of the blood, and grabs him gently by the shoulders.

"Hey," Eric says. "You okay?"

Eli is relieved that he is unable to smell Eric's blood. Otherwise, with his appetite being piqued, he may not be able to resist having a human in such close proximity of him.

"Yes," Eli says, forcing himself to relax and push the thoughts of live feeding from his mind.

"We'll walk away from it, okay? Come on," Eric says, nudging him towards the street.

They cross to the other side of the street, and Eli fights the urge to look back at the bleeding boy. When they are out of range from the blood scent's strongest concentration, Eli relaxes.

"Good job," Eric says. He gives Eli an encouraging pat on the back. "You handled that very well. How do you feel?"

"I feel fine," Eli says casually.

Eric stops him, forcing him to turn and face him. "Denial is not part of this process, Elias. Transparency is. This only works if you are honest with yourself, and with me."

Eli throws his head back and stares into the cloudy sky while biting his lower lip.

"Talk to me," Eric prods. "What are you feeling?"

Snuffing out the burning desire to flee Eric's side and plunge his fangs into the warm enticing meal he just passed up, Eli meets Eric's eyes. "You want transparency?"

Eric nods his head. "Transparency, at all times."

Eli's eyes narrow. If this were any other human, sober companion or not, he wouldn't dare let him know his true thoughts. Why should he? Humans are only concerned with keeping vampires restrained and placated. He's used to lying to them, to telling them what they want to hear so they'll give him a gold star and he can be on his merry way. The best method of survival in this post Human-Vampire War era is to go along with their demands, to agree to be corralled through rules and regulations like cattle through gates.

But Eli does not want to lie to Eric. He cannot. And if Eric really might be the reincarnation of Elizabeth in this lifetime, he is even more compelled to be open with him.

"I feel like I just put a nail in my own coffin," Eli answers.

Eric nods. "I've had other clients say the same thing. You feel that by denying yourself the live blood, that you're slowly killing yourself."

"Is that not what is happening, Eric? Let's be realistic. We live in a world now that views vampires as monsters when we eat live blood, yet that is our only true food source. If we want to live as free men, we are forced to go through rehab and transition over to synthetic blood, which is really just chemicals. It doesn't taste good, it weakens us, and there is nothing remotely satisfying about it. How is that living? How do you think it would feel if you had to willingly choose starvation and degradation just to be considered a free man?"

Eric silently curses the courts for putting him in this position. Since the incident with the vampire, he has harbored resentment and hatred towards the creatures. But before that, he had always been sensitive to their predicament. They were relentlessly discriminated against and looked down upon. Until the advent of vampire rights, society had long accepted and encouraged violence against vampires, all out of fear. Eric hates to admit it to himself, but he feels extremely sympathetic for Eli.

They continue walking down the street towards the sobriety meeting.

"Vampire policy is fraught with injustice," Eric says after some thought.

Eli laughs. "You might be the first non-activist human I've ever heard say that!"

Eric's face flushes as feelings of shame and confusion wash over him. He took part in his fair share of verbal vampire bashing after the incident that landed him this assignment.

"You are a complicated one, Eric Wayne," Eli marvels, watching his sober companion squirm from a hidden inner conflict. "Does transparency work both ways here?"

"What do you mean?"

They reach the location of the meeting and slowly walk up the cement steps leading to the entryway of the narrow brick building.

"You want me to be transparent, but will you do the same?"

Eric pulls open the heavy metal door and holds it open for Eli. "It doesn't work that way. As your sober companion it's my job to monitor your behavior and emotions and help you manage them to give you the best chance of avoiding a relapse."

Eli enters ahead of Eric. "What about as a friend?"

"I told you, we're not ... friends," Eric mumbles.

"Is that their rule, or yours?"

"Welcome! Are you here for the sobriety meeting?" A cheerful woman with bouncy red curls and rosy cheeks greets them in the echoing hallway.

"Yes," Eric answers, making his tone more professional. "This is Elias Alexander and I'm Eric, his sober companion."

"It is so nice to meet you, Eric!" She shakes his hand first, then turns to Eli. "Welcome, Elias! It is so important that you are here. We are so grateful that you have made the choice to go clean!"

"Thank you for having me," Eli says, nauseated by the woman's patronizing tone.

"Please, come in! We are about to start."

Eli and Eric follow the energetic woman into the meeting room with a circle of metal chairs arranged in its center. Only a few chairs are empty, a clear indication of the increasing popularity of the rehab program. Male and female vampires of differing ages at their time of change sit with their sober companions and chat while waiting for the meeting to start. Eli and Eric sit in the only two remaining empty chairs.

The curly red haired woman lightly claps her hands together to bring the room to order. "Hello everyone, my name is Amelia."

"Hello, Amelia," the group repeats.

"Amelia," Eric says. He eyeballs Eli for being silent but says nothing.

"I am so happy to have you all here once again. We have a new group member today! Elias and his sober companion Eric. Please give them a warm welcome!"

The group mumbles a collective welcome and Eric and Eli nod receptively. Eli is once again relieved that he cannot smell the blood of any of the human sober companions, including Amelia. Even he must admit the human chemical dosing is helpful to his plight.

"Let's get right to the sharing today, shall we? Does anyone want to go first?"

A nervous looking male vampire timidly holds up his hand. "I'd like to say something."

"Yes, Walter! Please go ahead!"

"Uh, hello, I'm Walter, and I'm a recovering live blood feeder."

"Hello, Walter," the group greets him.

"Walter," Eli says flatly. He glances at Eric for approval, but Eric is staring intently at the floor. Eli's eyes fall to Eric's hands. They're balled into fists with the thumbs tucked underneath the fingers. *Oddly familiar*, Eli thinks to himself. *Elizabeth used to make the same fists when she was uncomfortable with something. Could this really be her?*

Walter bumbles through his sob story of how he decided to stop drinking live blood. He is a young vampire, no more than 20 years old, in a 50 year old man's body. Eli feels no sympathy for him. Walter's trials and tribulations pale in comparison to Eli's millennium of living under the witch's curse to endure an endless cycle of heartache.

"Thank you, Walter," Amelia coos, encouraging the group to clap in support. "Can we hear from our newest member? Elias Alexander, would you like to share your story with us?"

Whispering erupts among the group members, both vampires and humans consorting with each other over the drop of the legendary vampire's name.

Eric looks up from the floor, his interest piqued at the prospect of hearing Eli's story. He suppresses a laugh while watching the stupefied group members murmur to each other. Eli's reputation precedes him.

Eli smiles politely. "Uh, not really, Amelia," he says.

"Don't be shy, Elias. We are all in this together. Sharing is crucial to your emotional healing!" Amelia says.

Eric raises an eyebrow, silently urging him to share. Eli cringes internally at the notion of sharing emotions with the apathetic group of strangers. Nevertheless, he clears his throat and conjures what he believes to be an acceptable offering. The group falls silent as they listen intently to the handsome celebrity vampire.

"Rehab was difficult, to say the least," he begins. "A part of me felt like I was dying." He shrugs his shoulders. "A part of me wanted to. But I have always had a reason to keep going in this life. So I chose to focus on that reason, and doing so got me through it."

"And what *was* your reason?" A female vampire, appearing to have been in her 40's when she was turned, asks with intense interest.

Eli smiles and his eyes fall to the floor as he imagines Elizabeth's smiling face.

"Love," a male vampire chimes in.

Eli looks up at him, surprised that he is such an easy study.

"It was love, wasn't it?" The vampire repeats.

Eli nods. "Yes. It was love."

The group sighs collectively, vampires and humans revealing the mutual driving force behind their own sobriety and life motivations.

"Is there a more noble reason than love?" Amelia comments.

"It has nothing to do with nobility," Eli says. "It is simply a matter of what you wouldn't do to see someone you love again. What you wouldn't do to be with them again. To see them smile. To touch them again. That was my lifeline."

"Thank you so much for sharing, Elias," Amelia says.

The group applauds him, and he flashes a quick smile. But his thoughts jump from Elizabeth to the sober companion at his side. He looks at Eric, who returns his glance with inquisitive eyes. Eli wants nothing more than to fight the notion that Elizabeth is back but as something different. In a thousand years, she has always reincarnated as the exact image of her original self. But this time?

When the meeting adjourns, Eli takes in a deep breath of the cool fall air as he and Eric trot down the stairs leading to the sidewalk. The group members pat him on the back or shake his hand as they spill out past him and he holds a small, plastic smile in place for their benefit, allowing it to fade as they disburse.

"Wow. Do we really have to do this every week?" Eli grumbles.

"Who is it?" Eric asks.

"Who is who?"

"The one you love, dork," Eric laughs. "A big bad vampire like you says you made it through rehab because of love. So, who is it?"

"Eric?" A woman's voice calls from behind them.

Eric turns around, his mouth falling half open. A young woman with short pale blonde hair and blue eyes approaches him carefully. She is dressed in a dark pantsuit and carries a leather brief case.

"Robin," Eric mumbles.

The two stare silently at each other for a long agonizing moment. Eli glances between the two, waiting for Eric to snap out of his stupor and introduce them.

"How are you?" Robin says finally.

Eric shrugs his shoulders. "I'm fine. How are you?" He notices a wedding band on her ring finger.

Robin forces a small smile, but it fades quickly. She looks at him with great concern.

In an effort to jump start a real conversation, Eli loudly clears his throat.

"Uh, sorry. Eli, this is Robin," Eric says his hand gesturing between the two. "Robin, Eli."

"Hello," Eli says with a slight bow and a smile.

Robin looks him up and down but doesn't return his greeting. Her eyes return to Eric.

"You're still working as a ..." Robin trails off, glancing at the vampire again.

"Sober companion, yes. Court ordered, remember?" Eric says. He fidgets awkwardly with his hands before shoving them into his coat pockets.

"Of course I remember. Well, I have to go, so ... it was nice seeing you," Robin says. Her face remains stoic, her eyes clouded with the emotions of their shared stormy past. She hurries past them, her pumps clicking on the sidewalk as she goes.

Unable to manage another word, Eric pulls a hand out of his

pocket and waves at her back, then smacks himself in the forehead with his palm. He starts walking slowly down the sidewalk, head drooping like Charlie Brown.

Eli holds up his hands expecting an explanation, but as Eric ambles farther away from him he realizes it won't come without encouragement. He jogs to catch up with the now sulking sober companion.

"What was *that*?" he says. "Is it just me, or was that the most awkward moment in the history of awkward moments?"

Eric grumbles and picks his head up long enough to gaze ahead of them at Robin as she disappears into a crowd crossing the street.

Eli playfully elbows him in the arm. "Well? Spill!"

"I'd rather not talk about it," Eric says. He glances over and chuckles when he sees Eli frowning emphatically, his dark brown eyes large and sad. "Aw, come on, it's nothing." Eric groans.

"Who's Robin, Eric? Who's Robin, eh?" Eli teases him, poking him in the arm until he relents.

"All right. But don't expect me to share any other details about my personal life with you," Eric says, glaring sternly.

"I expect nothing of the sort!" Eli says, holding up his right palm as if testifying in court.

"Robin was my fiancé."

"*Was*, huh? What happened?"

Eric walks on for several feet, then stops to face Eli. "It's like you said in the meeting. When you love someone that much, you'd do anything for them, right?"

"Of course," Eli says.

"That's what I had with Robin. At least, I thought I did. Then one day, something happened. I did something, for her, and she rejected me. She said she didn't want to marry someone capable of doing what I did. So she left."

"What did you do?"

Eric hesitates. "I can't tell you that. I'm actually prohibited by the court."

"Wow," Eli says. They begin walking again. "Must have been pretty bad."

"The point is, I did it to protect her. But she didn't see it that way."

"Sorry to hear that," Eli says.

"I thought she was the one, you know? But when she made the choice to leave me, I kind of felt relieved."

"Relieved?"

"Yeah. I wouldn't want to spend my life with someone that doesn't accept me for what I am."

Eli is floored. "You make it sound so easy," he says.

"What?"

He has spent the past thousand years continually wooing Elizabeth, only to have her repeatedly reject eternity with him because he is a vampire. And after only one failed relationship, Eric effortlessly sums up the barrage of inner doubts Eli has been plagued by with a simple sentence.

"I'm a bit envious of you, Eric," Eli says quietly.

"Envious? Why?"

He peers into his companion's clear blue eyes. They are full of hope despite being tainted with pain. If only his own hope were still as strong.

"You've already saved yourself years of pain by deciding to let go of something that cannot be."

"Doesn't mean it didn't hurt like hell," Eric says. "But I want to be accepted for what I am. I may end up walking the earth alone, thinking like that, right?" He says with a meek laugh.

"You're not alone," Eli says cheerfully. "You have me."

Two blocks from home, a small storefront catches Eli's eye.

"Hey, can we stop in here for a minute?" Eli asks.

Eric reads the store window and raises and eyebrow. "Seriously? A magic shop?"

"Well, it's not all magic, per se," Eli says, opening the door and walking in. They are immediately accosted by the heavy scent of incense. "It's kind of an alternative religious place too," Eli says.

Eric wrinkles his nose in an attempt to prevent a sneezing fit. "Alternative religion. Okay," he says.

Eli begins wandering through the aisles intently studying the contents on every shelf. Candles. Crystals. Potions. Magic books.

"Oh my goodness! We know you!" A man's chipper voice comes from the back of the shop. "Honey, look! It's Elias Alexander!"

A gasp comes from under the back counter and a woman pops her head up. "No way! He's here?"

"Do you know them?" Eric asks Eli. The couple drop their tasks and bolt out from behind the counter towards Eli.

"Uh, no, I don't know these people," Eli whispers.

The young hippie couple in their mid-twenties nearly bowl Eli over as they reach for his hands and shake them fervently. He smiles and laughs nervously, unsure of what he's supposed to do.

"I can't believe it's really you!" the young man says.

"I can't either! This is so amazing!" the woman agrees.

The couple hop up and down and squeal like fan girls. Noticing Eli's puzzled expression, the young man stops jumping and gives Eli his hand back.

"Sorry, Elias, we are just so excited to see you. Since you moved into the neighborhood, our sales have quadrupled! We were going out of business, but when the *New York Times* printed the article about you being in town, people just went nuts and started getting into magic and alternative lifestyles again!"

The woman squeaks. "Yes! You saved our business!" She gasps loudly and looks at her husband. "Oh, my god. We should totally, like, give him a present!"

Eli holds up his hands and waves them gently. "No, no please. You do not need to give me anything."

"It would be an honor, Mr. Alexander," the young man says

seriously. "Is there something you are interested in?"

Eli cocks his head. "You have any old books on curses? Witchcraft?" He ignores Eric's inquisitive glance.

The couple think hard for a moment. "No, but we may be able to special order you something," the young man says.

"Oh! Our witchery supply is a bit lacking right now, but we do have this," the young woman says, retrieving a sharp stone dagger from a glass case by the cash register.

"What is that?" Eli says, taking it from her to examine it.

The couple exchange a tense look, glance around the empty shop for witnesses, and lean in.

"We believe it to be the only item that can *kill* a witch," the young woman whispers.

"Yeah, we don't like to say it out loud and risk offending anyone," the young man says, eyes darting around and nodding nervously. "You never know what kind of mystical creatures could be walking around."

"Mystical creatures?" Eric says, amused. "You mean besides vampires?"

"Precisely," the couple says in unison.

"Yeah, we believe in fair treatment for all beings, no matter who they are."

Eli grunts in approval. "Cool." He hands the stone dagger back to the young woman. "Uh, you hang on to this for now. I'll think about it."

"You got it," the young man says. "We'll hold it for you. And if you think of a spell book or anything else you'd like us to order, you know how to find us!"

The young woman replaces the stone dagger and grabs their business cards from the counter. She hands one to Eli and Eric.

"This is us, Nathan and Diane. You can call us any time, we live upstairs so we're always available. Both of our cell phones and email address are on there, so don't be a stranger, Elias! You and your mate here are welcome any time!"

"My name is Eric," Eric says.

Nathan and Diane both accost Eli with handshakes again.

"Elias, you and your mate Eric are welcome any time. Please come back and see us soon!" Nathan gushes.

"Sober companion," Eric mumbles, feeling the couple's ecstatic state is too distracting for a real introduction.

Eli chuckles. "Thank you so much, Nathan and Diane. I may be calling upon you soon."

"Oh, please do! That would be wonderful!"

Eric is the first out the door and holds it open, waiting for Eli to peel himself away from the giddy hippie couple.

Eli shoots him a look as he comes out. "They know me," he says, lifting his chin up in a half gloat.

Eric snorts. "Are you sure that's a good thing?"

That night, after Eric goes to bed, Eli plants himself at the desk in the small downstairs study filled with his collection of hardback books on witches, curses, and magic lore. It's one of hundreds of nights he has spent scrutinizing the books, line by line, desperate to find a way to break Elizabeth's curse. Eric's sudden appearance in his life fills him with a heightened sense of urgency. He fears it is a sign that Elizabeth could be lost to him forever.

After spending fruitless hours on the pursuit, Eli growls in frustration and throws the hefty book of curses against the wall. Several of its delicate yellowed pages flitter out as the book crashes to the floor. He stares at the mess, recalling the last time he lost his cool and threw the same book. It was in front of Elizabeth, only he didn't know she had been watching.

It's 1961. Boston. He just threw the spell book against the wall of the small apartment he and Elizabeth have been staying in. He rubs his face heavily and slides his fingers through his dark hair.

"What is it, Elias?" Elizabeth's voice comes from behind him.

He turns to see her approach him from the bedroom, looking as beautiful as ever. Her long blond hair is disheveled and she rubs her eyes sleepily as she walks towards him. Her white nightgown hits just above her knees revealing shapely legs and her small feet fall softly on the soft carpeted floor as she walks.

"I am sorry I woke you," Eli says warmly. He holds open his arms and she falls into them, sitting on his lap.

She examines the books on his desk, shuffling them around as she reads the titles. "Still looking for your cure?"

"Either a cure for me, or a cure for you," he says.

She shifts on his lap so she can see his face. "Which do you think it will be?"

"I do not hold out hope that I can be cured," he says as he gently caresses her hair. "I only hope to be able to break the curse upon you."

"I choose to believe you about the curse," she says. "You've shown me what you are, and while it scares me, it also opens to me the possibility that I truly will die soon."

Eli looks away, pained to hear her speak the words. She slowly guides his chin back to look him in the eyes.

"But I have also come to love you more than I ever thought was possible. The feelings I have with you are so deep and true. I cannot imagine a life without you."

"You don't have to! Elizabeth, I may not be able to break the curse upon your life. But I can give you a new one! We can be together, forever!"

Elizabeth sighs. "Only by making me what you are."

"I know it is not what you want to hear, but it is all I can do to keep us together! I love you so much." He pulls her into a firm, tender kiss.

"Just love me now," she says.

Their attraction ignites and he picks her up as he stands. They kiss passionately, her skin flushing as her body heats up. He fights the urge to feed on her, as he always has, yet the yearning is always there. He fantasizes that it would be pure ecstasy to not only make love to her, but at the same time to ingest her blood and the emotions carried by it. But out of respect for her wishes, he keeps himself from feeding.

He brings her into their small dark bedroom and lays her on the bed, covering her in kisses while reveling in her moans and the way her body squirms *beneath him as she anticipates their lovemaking. He teases her more and when he finally enters her, the tightness of her body and the breathy moan that escapes her throat sends him over the edge.*

The beast within him fights to escape, but he must hold back most of his strength to avoid hurting her as he thrusts hungrily into her. He roughly kisses her neck, keeping his lips drawn tight over the fangs that have jutted out from the excitement. Over her choppy breaths and swelling moans, her heartbeat pounds in his ears. Her throat's pulse pounds beneath his lips and the intoxicating aroma of her blood and pheromones speeds him to the point of climax.

"Eli?"

Ripped from the sultry memory, Eli jumps out of the chair, fangs out, breathing heavy.

Eric, in a sleeveless T-shirt and shorts, stares at him from the doorway with an eyebrow raised. His tousled hair and the red lines on his cheek indicate he had been sound asleep when Eli lost it and slammed the book against the wall.

"What?" Eli says, embarrassed. Aware that his fangs are out, he covers his mouth and wills himself to calm down so they will retract.

"I heard a loud crash," Eric says, looking down at the book. "Is there a reason you're throwing books at three in the morning?" He bends down to pick up the book and the loose pages, reading the title. "You're reading about witchcraft?"

Eli grabs the book and loose pages from him and tosses them on the desk. "Sorry, didn't mean to raise a ruckus," he says, letting out a sheepish chuckle.

Eric's eyes widen and he waits for further explanation, but Eli just stands with his mouth covered.

"Okay, then," Eric says. "I'm going back to bed." He starts to turn, but snaps back and points a finger. "You're not relapsing, are you?"

"Hmm-mm," Eli says, adamantly shaking his head and keeping his mouth covered.

Eric glares at him. "I'm going to test you in the morning," he warns.

"Uh-huh, fine."

"Okay. Well, good night. Or, whatever," Eric says. He sleepily ruffles his hair and turns, and Eli again sees the mark on his shoulder.

Eli speeds over to him, grabbing his arm. The cold shock of seeing the mark again sends his fangs into immediate retraction. "What is this?" He asks.

Eric glances down at his shoulder, then at Eli, curious about his serious and concerned expression.

"It's a birthmark," Eric says slowly. Eli holds his arm, squinting as he examines the mark. "Is something wrong?"

"You've always had it then?"

"Uh, yeah! Hence the term *birthmark*!"

"Sorry. It's just … unique." An image of Elizabeth's arm bearing the same mark flashes through his mind. He looks into Eric's bloodshot eyes. "I knew someone that had a similar birthmark."

An aggressive frustration begins to simmer inside him. It is a volatile mix of hunger for live blood and the sexual tension lingering from his vivid memory of making love to Elizabeth, interrupted by Eric.

Eric. What I wouldn't give to smell his blood right now, Eli thinks to himself.

"Can I have my arm back now?" Eric says, his cool tone splintering Eli's focus.

"Sorry," he says and releases his hold.

"Hey," Eric says, looking him intently in the eye. "You having a rough night?"

"I don't know." Eli turns and paces away. "Maybe."

"Do you want to eat? It may take the edge off." Eli considers the idea but doesn't answer. "Come on," Eric says. He leads him into the kitchen and takes out a pint of synthetic blood from the refrigerator. He opens it and pours it into a ceramic mug, microwaving it to warm it up. "Sit," he orders the seemingly disgruntled vampire.

Eli sits at the table. "Thank you," he says. Eric places the warmed synthetic blood in front of him and sits across from him. He fiddles with the mug, turning it around in circles by the handle.

"Talk to me," Eric says. He leans back in his chair, crossing his arms. "What's got you so riled up?"

"What makes you think I'm riled up?" Eli takes a sip of the warm chemical concoction.

"Well, let's see. It's the middle of the night and you're throwing things. And you seem to have a sudden odd paranoia about birthmarks," Eric adds with a grin. "Was the meeting hard for you? It will get easier."

"It's not the meeting," Eli says.

"Okay."

Eli takes another sip and grimaces. "This stuff really is horrible."

"Oh it can't be that bad," he says, grabbing the mug. "You know, I've always wondered what it tastes like."

"You won't like it!" Eli warns.

Eric takes a sip, his face contorting. He chokes as he swallows the small amount of liquid and shoves the mug back at the vampire. "Oh, my god!" He says, coughing and wiping his mouth with the back of his hand. "You're serious! That tastes like shit!"

Eli bursts into laughter. "I told you!"

"What the hell? How do they expect you to live on that?"

"Welcome to my world," Eli chuckles. He swallows down the rest of the thick red liquid and cringes. "Now do you understand why this is so controversial? Vampires can hardly stand the stuff, yet if we want to win our legal freedom in this country, we have to exist on it. It is …"

"An atrocity," Eric says, his voice dropping into sadness. "Eli, I'm sorry. I really had no idea."

"It is the state of the union, I'm afraid," Eli says. "What other choice is there?"

"You could have stayed underground. You would have been illegal, but at least you would have more freedom."

"Freedom to do what? Feed on live blood? In exchange for what? A lifetime spent running from the human authorities? No," he says, leaning back. "I've done that, Eric. It has its perks, but I got tired of it. Now, I want peace more than anything."

"Enslavement to human law is peace to you?"

"Everyone is a slave to the law, Eric. Every culture, every society has their rules. Deviants are persecuted. It's the nature of civilization."

"That doesn't mean it can't be improved upon. Vampire-Americans are discriminated against more than any cultural group in history. You have rights, just like anyone else does."

"I don't disagree with you, Eric. Even though the war is over, it is still fresh in our minds. It will be generations before the pain of it begins to dissipate."

"Have you ever thought about using your status in the vampire community to become an advocate? Help push things along?"

Eli chuckles. "I've spent too many years on the other side of things, Eric. To many, I am viewed as villainous."

"Things change," Eric says. "People change. Vampires can change too. You don't seem like a villain to me."

Eli looks warmly at his sober companion. "You are a true idealist. The ever-hopeful Eric Wayne," he says.

"Hopeful, yeah. But I'm far from … perfect. My penance here is …" He stops himself.

"Penance?"

Eric shakes his head, fatigue showing on his face. "I need more sleep," he says, standing from the table. He pats the vampire on the shoulder as he passes. "Take it easy the rest of the night. I'll see you when the sun comes up."

"What is your age?" Eli asks abruptly.

Eric stops in the kitchen's doorway. "My age? I'm twenty five. Why?" He gazes drowsily back at Eli, who continues to face away from him.

"When is your birthday?"

"In the spring. Why do you ask?"

"Just curious," Eli says. "Good night."

Dread fills Eli's heart.

Chapter Five

Later that same night, a monumental gathering of vampires convenes inside the dank bellows of an abandoned Brooklyn warehouse. The windows are blackened with spray paint and heavy log chains with padlocks secure each door. Guard vampires dressed like Secret Service agents secure the perimeter inside and out. An oblong conference table sets in the center of the oil-stained cement floor with eleven captain's chairs for the vampire leaders. Their cohorts sit scattered around them on metal chairs, boxes, and crates. The scene is akin to a meeting of mafia bosses and their men, but no humans occupy this premises.

Low chattering among vampires ceases as one stands up to formally begin the meeting.

"My brothers and sisters. Thank you for attending on such short notice. We are at the precipice of change."

The speaker, one of the original vampires, is a man turned in his thirty fifth year of life. Despite his youthful looks, with stylish dark blonde hair and striking blue eyes amplified by the electric blue tie around his neck, his words are charged with wisdom and intent.

"We are honored to be here, Castor," a male vampire responds, nodding out of respect.

"The de-evolution of vampires in this country must come to an end. Plans are in place to upset the human constructs preventing us from flourishing."

The warehouse erupts with a soundtrack of whispers.

"I understand many of you have concerns. I will hear them now." Castor sits at the head of the table, opening the floor for discussion.

An elder vampire at the table clears his throat to voice his opinion. "With all due respect, Castor. We risk losing all progress made since the Human-Vampire War. Any act of opposition will be seen as a violation of the law. We will lose even more ground and risk persecution for it."

Many vampires nod in agreement and eagerly await a response from their leader.

"A valid point, Nikola," Castor says. "Which is why our methods will begin as a covert form of political warfare. We will systematically destroy the very institution the humans have designed to keep us enslaved. It will appear to them as if their system is fatally flawed, calling for the necessity of new legislation. Key players are already in place within the federal and local legal systems to facilitate our efforts. Judges. Law enforcement. Politicians. Top political leaders. There exists a staggering number of vampire sympathizers among humans, and for the past two decades, we have worked to harness and align these forces, all in preparation of the new beginning."

"What guarantee do we have of our safety? If the plan fails, what resources are in place to fall back upon?"

Castor lets out a dry chuckle. "Our plan cannot fail. It is hundreds of years in the making. Make no mistake, ladies and gentlemen. Our course into a bright new millennium has been charted against the stars. The time has come to seize control of our destiny as the superior race."

A female vampire sitting at the table stands briefly. "What about our brothers and sisters that have undergone blood rehab? Do they stand with us, or should we consider them to be human sympathizers?"

"We will liberate them. They are, after all, our family. I do not believe one of our kind would willingly continue to exist on synthetic when it is no longer mandated," Castor says.

"Elias Alexander," a lower level vampire says from the back of the crowd. Whispers again rumble through the group. The vampire stands and walks towards the table.

"Jeremiah," Castor says. "What is your concern with Elias Alexander?"

"He is making a fool out of us," Jeremiah says. "What do we do about him?"

"I am glad you mention him, Jeremiah. In fact, you may be interested to know that Elias Alexander is the first step in our plan of revolution."

"How so? He is already rehabilitated. He doesn't even drink live anymore!" Another male vampire calls out.

"Precisely. A vampire of Elias Alexander's stature will always turn into headline news. So when he purposely and severely relapses, the entire blood rehab and sobriety program will collapse on itself. His transgression will lead and inspire others, and he will unwittingly become the public face of relapse. His will be the face of the failed institution constructed by humans. There will be backlash of epic proportions. Vampire rights activists will be outraged when they learn from Elias Alexander that permanent rehab is just not possible, and it is in fact cruel and unusual punishment, something even the most conservative Americans will not tolerate. After Elias's fall from grace, the politics will change. That is where I come in. I am to be elected to the New York State Senate next fall and I will systematically rewrite vampire legislation from within."

"We have full confidence in your abilities, Castor," the vampire Nikola says. "How can you ensure Elias' relapse? And furthermore, how can you base the future of our race upon one vampire's transgression?"

Castor laughs, this time a guttural, boisterous howl. "You think too little of me, Nikola. Elias Alexander will be the public face of rehab failure. But I have already given the order for operations to begin to destroy the manufacturing process of synthetic blood, along with the chemicals the humans use to mask their blood scent. Hungry, rehabilitated vampires and their sober companions will riot. Massacres will erupt, and blame will be placed not upon vampires, no, for they were just hungry and have a right to eat! No, the humans responsible for allowing the synthesization process to fail will be held accountable for bloodshed. Vampires will be regarded as a persecuted, downtrodden race and something must be done about it! The public will demand it."

"And with you in the Senate to rewrite the law, we cannot fail this time," the female vampire adds.

"After next year's election, vampires will be the majority race in the Senate, and the House," Castor says. "Political warfare at its finest, ladies and gentlemen."

The vampires loudly applaud Castor, some whooping and whistling their support.

"There is just one more item I will need your help with," Castor says, patting the air with his hands to hush the group.

"Anything to help the cause," Nikola says.

"We must flood the blood rehabilitation programs with vampires. The more vampires that fail rehab after Elias Alexander leads the way, the better our cause will look. I want you and your families to join programs. Make it look good. These are the last days we bow down to human policy."

"We concur, Castor," Nikola says. "It will be done."

Applause erupts again, and the vampire meeting concludes.

Jeremiah makes his way through the dispersing crowd to Castor. "Castor, if you need help with Elias Alexander, consider me at your beck and call."

A woman steps out from behind Castor. She has been sitting off to his side, away from the table during the meeting. She is not a vampire, but her scent is not human either. Clad in a long black and maroon dress, her long brown hair sits well below her shoulders. She sets her dark blue eyes upon Jeremiah and smiles.

"Your help is greatly appreciated, Jeremiah," she says, extending a hand out to him.

"My pleasure, Madam," Jeremiah says.

"Come, my dear," Castor says, holding out his arm for the woman to take. "Let us watch the sunrise together."

Chapter Six

"Waffles?"

Eric rustles from his sleep and looks in the direction of the voice to see Eli leaning in the doorway of his bedroom holding a ceramic mug.

"What?" Eric mumbles groggily.

"Do you like them?"

"Do I like what?" Eric sits up and squints at his watch.

"Waffles. Because I just made the most perfect looking waffles on the planet," Eli says, holding his head high with pride.

"Uh. Yeah, I guess so." Eric clumsily throws his legs over the bed, unaware one of his feet is tangled in the sheet until he stands and tries to take a step and stumbles. He catches himself in time to keep from face planting onto the hard floor.

"Wow," Eli remarks. "You are not a morning person, are you?"

Eric grumbles and shuffles past the chipper vampire. "I hate mornings."

"Well, in any event. The world's most perfect waffles await you. Then we must be off to work."

"To work? Another case?" Eric calls from the bathroom

before shutting the door.

"Another case, but these bodies aren't so fresh."

"Oh?"

"I won't spoil your breakfast, come down when you're ready," Eli says jogging down the stairs.

Eli reads the morning newspaper for the third time while Eric finishes off the waffles.

"Oh, wow. Did you see that?" Eric says.

Eli folds the paper down. "See what?"

"There, the front page headline. A new vampire rights bill is being introduced in the House. That's good, right?"

"It will never pass," Eli says. He folds the newspaper and tosses it on the table.

"What makes you say that?"

Eli sips his mug of warm synthetic blood. "It is just for show. Nothing will come of it."

"Yeah, but there's a chance, right? It's in the House, so maybe …"

"If you read the fine print, it is attached to another bill that calls for mandatory healthcare reform. It is essentially bogus. Someone just wants to make things look like vampire rights are progressing, but they're not."

Eric stares into his coffee. "Doesn't that bother you?"

Eli shrugs. "When you have lived as long as I have, you learn what issues are to be ignored."

"So you choose apathy over action?"

"Apathy and survival are not the same thing, Eric."

Eric stands and collects his dishes, bringing them to the sink. The insidious cleaning ensues.

"If it were me, I just think I'd feel better trying to improve things, rather than just watching the world pass by me."

He glances over his shoulder and is surprised to see Eli staring at him with a crooked grin.

"What?"

Eli joins him at the sink and watches in amusement as Eric mercilessly scrubs the fork. "You seem to have a genuine interest in civil rights. Why are you working as a sober companion?"

"I told you, I'm court ordered to do this job," Eric mumbles. He attacks the spoon next.

"Okay, but what were you doing before you were *court ordered* to do this?"

"Law school," he says.

"Really? You wanted to be a lawyer? Why did you quit?"

Eric finishes exorcising the dirt from the dishes and shuts off the faucet. He dries his hands and smirks at the vampire.

"Can't tell you that, Eli. Sorry."

Eli shrugs. "Okay. The mysterious Eric Wayne strikes again."

Thirty minutes later they arrive at the waterfront crime scene. The chilly but sunny morning would be enjoyable if it weren't for the presence of dead bodies. Captain Meyers smokes a cigar and chats with an evidence technician as Eli approaches.

"Captain," Eli greets.

"Vampire," Captain Meyers says curtly. He points at three bodies wrapped in heavy clear plastic. "These sad sacks were pulled from the water this morning. I thought we'd give you a chance to see if you can figure anything out before we take them in."

The evidence technician hands Eli and Eric a pair of latex gloves.

Eric waves him off, saying "I don't need these, I'm not -"

"Yes, he does," Eli says, nodding for the technician to give Eric the gloves. "Come on," he says.

Eric nervously shoves his hands into the gloves. He feels a light wave of nausea creep over him as he dreads coming any closer to the dead bodies.

"Eli, I really don't want to see this."

"I need your help," Eli says. "Come on."

Eli looks at the three plastic wrapped bodies and kneels next to one of them. He takes a knife from his coat pocket and slices through the plastic, careful not to cut the skin.

"Hold this open, please," Eli says.

Eric reluctantly kneels down, coughing and covering his nose as the rotten smell of the decomposing body hits his nostrils.

"Just like this," Eli says.

Eric holds his breath and cringes as he holds the plastic open long enough for Eli to make a small incision in the dead man's neck. He shoves a gloved finger into the cut and moves it around inside, trying to collect a sample of blood. When he withdraws his finger only a small beaded trail of blood shows up.

"Is that enough?"

"Yes, it should be," Eli says. "You can let go now."

"Good, 'cause I'm about to lose my waffles," Eric says, standing up and backpedaling away from the body. He coughs again and spins, gulping for fresh air.

Eli chuckles at his reaction.

"You think it's appropriate to laugh at a time like this, vampire?" Captain Meyers says.

"No. I apologize, Captain," Eli says.

Captain Meyers glares at Eric and gestures for Eli to hurry up. "Well? Come on, get it over with. Tell me what I need to know so I don't have to see your face anymore."

"Hey what the hell is your problem?" Eric says angrily. "Your attitude really sucks!"

Captain Meyers strides to Eric and leers in his face. "What'd you say to me?"

"Eric," Eli says, standing up.

"I said your attitude sucks! Eli solved a murder for you last night, and he's about to do it again. You've been nothing but a dick to him!"

Captain Meyers grabs Eric by the collar. "I don't give a damn about freaks like him," he growls. "We're better off without them. If I weren't mandated by my superiors to use him I would have nothing to do with him, or any pansy ass vampire sympathizer like *you*!"

"You take that back, you son of a bitch!" Eric yells.

Eli steps between them, pushing Eric back. "Eric, calm down," he warns. "Captain, I apologize."

The Captain's face is flushed with rage. "Normally I'd tell the human to keep you on a leash, vampire! But this time, you better get this little vampire lover under control or I'll bust both your asses!"

"What the hell, Captain?" Eric yells again.

"Understood," Eli says. He turns to Eric and forces him to step back. "Stop it, Eric!"

Eric whirls, chest heaving with anger. "I hate his attitude," Eric grumbles. "He's such a bigot!"

"What did you say the night Jeremiah attacked me?" Eli says, angering.

"What?"

"The night Jeremiah attacked me. You forget already? You said 'Damn it, I hate vampires.'"

"That was different, Eli, he -"

"Was it? How?"

Eric realizes his own hypocrisy and relents. "Ahh," he grumbles. "I'm sorry, Eli. That was wrong of me."

"Wait over there, and stop provoking the Captain of the NYPD, will you?" Eli returns to the bodies. "Sorry, Captain. Won't happen again," he says. "I'll get this done."

Eric watches as Eli swabs for another blood sample with the evidence technician's help. As per the night before, he dabs the dead blood on the tip of his tongue and waits for the residual memories and emotions to manifest. Eli stands and walks to the waterfront, strolling slowly as he sees into the dead man's past. When he turns to face the Captain, a terse expression plays across his features.

"Captain," Eli says.

"What was it? A mob hit? Loan sharks?" The Captain says, puffing on his newly lighted cigar.

"These three men were sober companions. This was a

vampire hate crime. My guess is, the vampires these men were assigned to are also dead. You should be able to identify them by contacting the board. I'll draw a sketch of the killers, and email it to you by this afternoon."

"Vampire hate crime, huh," the Captain says, seeming relieved. "Well, that's unfortunate."

Eric overhears the verdict and angers at the Captain's lack of empathy. Aware of his agitation, Eli glares at him to ensure he stays silent.

"All right then. Boys, let's get these guys to the morgue." The Captain saunters back to a patrol car with another police officer.

Eli removes his gloves and hands them to the evidence technician. "Thanks, Jim," he says.

"No problem, Eli. Good work," Jim says.

Eric watches as the Captain is driven away in his chariot. "What a jerk," he grumbles.

Eli gives him the cold shoulder as they leave the crime scene. After twenty minutes of silence, Eric's guilt gets the better of him.

"Hey," he says, jogging to catch up with Eli's speedy walk. "I really am sorry. I hope I didn't blow it for you back there."

Eli remains silent and maintains his speed.

"Look, I'll make it right with the Captain. He doesn't need another excuse to treat you like shit."

Eli stops and turns too fast for Eric to see and he plows into him.

"Do you like museums?" Eli says, gazing around thoughtfully.

"Museums? Uh, I guess so, why?"

Eli is already speeding in a new direction. Eric dodges pedestrians and cars as he scurries to catch up to the impulsive vampire.

"Where are we going?"

"You will see," Eli says, grinning as Eric runs into a surly New Yorker who curses him.

"Sorry, Sir," Eric stammers. "Hey, wait up!"

Minutes later, they arrive at the Museum of Natural History. Its four floors of gallery space span several city blocks. Inside, the museum hosts exhibits covering the varying disciplines of human science, with the most recent pertaining to the discovery of vampires and the aftermath of the decades-long Human-Vampire War.

"Have you ever been here?" Eli asks.

"No, I haven't," Eric says. "Always wanted to though."

After showing his temporary Vampire Visa to the security guards, Eli makes a donation at the welcome desk, and they begin the tour of the museum. Of particular interest to both vampire and sober companion are the exhibits that cover the 1960's to the present, where the history of strife between humans and vampires is detailed with poignant statues, pictures, newspaper clippings, and scenes from the highlights of the war.

Eli stops in front of a life-sized model of a vampire with labels covering it head-to-toe detailing the anatomy of a vampire to demonstrate how vampires are different than humans. Eric joins him and studies the model.

"Marked and labeled like an animal in autopsy," Eli says grimly.

Eric sneaks a glance at Eli's expression and sees how much the display disturbs him. "It's a bit gruesome, if you ask me," Eric says. "I think vampires should be seem more as mythical creatures. Unique and beautiful."

"People forget that we were once human. We are not so different."

"I know. You're a type of evolution, Eli."

Eli looks at him. "When are you going to tell me what is giving you such a conflicted opinion about us?"

Eric drops his head. "Eli, I told you, I can't. I'm not -"

" - allowed, you told me, but I think you want to."

"And why do you think that?"

"Because being alone with a secret can destroy you," Eli says, shrugging when Eric glances at him with sorrow in his eyes. "You do not have to walk alone in life, Eric. It is okay to open up and lean on people when you need to."

Eric shakes his head and leans in to say in a hushed voice, "If you knew what I've done, you might think differently."

"Differently about opening up, or about you?"

"About me."

Eli raises an eyebrow. "I am intrigued," he says, smiling.

"You shouldn't be," Eric says, turning his attention back to the exhibit.

Eli laughs harder than he intends.

"What's so funny?"

"You are," he says. His laughter continues despite Eric's increasing agitation.

"Is everything a joke to you?"

"Not at all, Eric," he says, laughter trailing off. "I cannot imagine you have done anything worse than I myself have. I have been alive over a thousand years, remember? Do you not think I have probably committed more than my fair share of sin?"

Eric grins. "Have you? What, are you Vlad the Impaler or something?"

Eli erupts into laughter again. "Do you see an exhibit for Vlad the Impaler here?" Eli looks around pointedly. "Vlad the Impaler? Has anyone seen Vlad the Impaler here?" He announces loudly.

"Shut up, you jerk! You'll get us thrown out!" Eric says, trying not to laugh.

An elderly couple walking by looks at them and the man steps towards Eli. "I think there's more vampire things over there," he says, pointing a wrinkled hand towards the next exhibit hall. "They might have Vlad down there, but I can't really be sure, son."

Eli gives the elderly man a courteous bow and smiles. "Thank you, sir. I appreciate your help." He waits for the elderly couple to mosey away before giving Eric an ornery look.

"Nice," Eric says, faking his disapproval.

"This way, young man! To Vlad!" Eli says, bowing deeply and sweeping his arm in the direction of the hallway.

"You're ridiculous," Eric says, unable to hold his laughter any longer.

That afternoon, Eric hovers over Eli's shoulder in the study watching him sketch an image of the two men who killed the three sober companions.

"That's remarkable," Eric says.

"Thanks. But it took me hundreds of years to get this good," Eli says. "It really comes in handy with this job. And, there we go." He holds up the sketchbook. "You are looking at the faces of murderers."

"Are they human?"

"Yes. Humans full of hatred. These people are extremely dangerous. They will kill their own kind just for associating with vampires. This even makes my skin crawl." Eli shudders. He carefully tears the page from the booklet and places it on the flat scanner attached to his laptop.

"Captain Meyers should be pleased to see that," Eric says.

"One would hope."

With Eli busy at the computer, Eric picks up the sketchbook and flips through Eli's other sketches.

"Who is she?"

"Hmm?" Eli glances up from the computer and jumps when he sees Eric looking at the sketches of Elizabeth. He races over to keep him from flipping the next page, but is too late.

"You drew me?" Eric says, studying the near perfect charcoal sketch of himself on the page. "It's a perfect likeness."

Eli snatches the sketchbook from his hands. "Uh, yeah. It is something I do when I am bored and you were ... sleeping."

Eric smiles at him. "Wow. I've only been here a few days and you're already drawing pictures of me. You're not a serial killer, are you?"

"Not anymore," Eli says.

Eric waits for Eli to make light of his comment, but decides to change the subject when he doesn't.

"So, who's the girl? Is she the love of your life you talked about in group meeting?"

"Something like that," Eli says.

"Tell me about her." He plops down in an oversized chair next to the desk and casually crosses his arms over his chest.

"I would rather not, Eric," Eli says carefully.

Eric throws his hands up. "Okay. Something else then."

"Tell me something about you," Eli says. "And not just small talk. It has to be something of sustenance."

"If you're trying to get me to talk about why I'm court ordered to be a sober companion ..."

"No. Nothing off limits. How about this: you answer one of my questions, and in exchange I will answer one of yours. Deal?"

Eric leans his head back and consults the ceiling for advice. "Deal."

"All right." Eli clears his throat. "Would you ever choose to become a vampire?"

Eric snorts. "That's your question?"

"What? It's a perfectly good question! It's not too soft, not too hard. You said we had a deal, so ... would you?"

Eric agonizes over the question before arriving at a reasonable answer. "I don't think I would."

"Why not? You would be immortal. Live to see the future of mankind, of vampirekind. You could do anything you ever dreamed of with no time restrictions. How could you say no to that?"

"Because how could I possibly enjoy all of that alone?"

"You think you would be alone?"

Eric shrugs. "People don't stay together anymore. Everyone scatters in the wind, doing their own thing. Greed and lust and hunger for whatever satiates, drives people to the wrong ends. No bond seems to hold up for very long. I wouldn't want to spend eternity being left behind."

"Were the situation such that you had someone to spend it with, would you choose eternity then?"

"It would depend on the someone."

"I see," Eli says, gaze drifting to the floor.

"My turn," Eric says, energy returning to his voice. "What were you like before you decided to enter rehab and play by human rules?"

"Wow. You have no idea what you are asking."

"Is that off limits?"

"Well, no."

"Okay. Let's have it."

Eli sighs heavily. "All right. I am a vampire of my word."

Eric relaxes into the chair expecting a lengthy story.

"I was turned into a vampire at age twenty nine, over a thousand years ago. My oldest friend is nearly as old as I. I know who Dracula is. I actually spent some good quality time with the fellow."

Eric's mouth opens but he holds his tongue.

"Over the past millennium I have started forty five revolutions, overthrown thirty six governments, been banished from twenty five countries and sentenced to death one hundred and six times, mostly by idiot kings who felt threatened by a sideways glance," he says with a knowing laugh. "I'd rather not say how many humans or vampires I have killed. Most recently, I turned in a large group of fairly powerful vampires in Boston in exchange for asylum with the United States government, and a chance to enter the witness relocation program and go through blood rehab, so I can walk about feely in this great country without having to be concerned about such annoyances as being captured, tortured, and subsequently murdered by humans."

Eric stares at him wide-eyed.

"Does that answer your question, or do I need to elaborate?"

"Just one thing," Eric says. "How many people have you

turned into vampires?"

Eli blinks, stunned by Eric's disinterest in his historical account. "After everything I just said, your only question is how many vampires I have made?"

"I want to hear more details, of course," Eric says, now leaning forward in the chair. "But ... yeah, how many vampires have you made?"

"I think we'll stop there," Eli says, standing up. He picks the cell phone up from the desk and sends a text to the Captain. "Good, Captain Meyers got the sketch. The manhunt is on."

"Eli," Eric says, curious about his reluctance to answer the question. "Just give me a number. I won't judge."

"Won't you?" Eli counters.

"Come on."

"There is no number to give you, Eric."

"You mean ... you've never turned anyone?"

"No."

"But, don't you feel alone? I mean, where's this girl you mentioned? You draw her picture. You say she's the reason you made it through rehab. Is she ... is she dead?"

Eli meets his inquisitive gaze. "I cannot answer that, Eric."

"You can't answer? Or you won't answer?"

"I cannot."

"But that doesn't make sense. How can you not know if she's alive or dead?"

The alarm on Eric's wrist watch beeps, interrupting his interrogation. He pushes the button to make it stop and as he takes his hand away, both notice the severe trembling.

"Why are your hands shaking like that?" Eli asks.

Eric clasps his hands together to hide the symptoms. "Uh. It's time for my injection," he says, standing up fast and heading for the stairs. "You should eat now."

Eli detects a hint of Eric's blood smell as he hurries away. The chemicals beginning to wear off at the 24 hour mark. His thoughts turn hazy as hunger sets in and he heads to the kitchen to retrieve a pint of synthetic. Simply from smelling the faint scent of Eric's blood circulating in the air, the aggressive frustration simmers inside him again. He chugs down the cold pint of chemicals to quell the impending urge and finds himself returning to the forbidden thought of what Eric's blood tastes like. What memories would he see if he were to drink from him? Would he see Elizabeth's memories too? What would that feel like?

Eli returns to his study and picks up his sketchbook, slowly flipping through the dozens of sketches of Elizabeth. So as not to smudge the charcoal, he runs his hand gingerly over the outline of her face and smiles. His hands flip the remainder of the pages until landing on the sketch of Eric, his face captured in a timeless portrait. Eli stares at the drawing, still not wanting to admit to himself that the tides have indeed turned, and something has disrupted Elizabeth's reincarnation cycle. But what?

A loud crash tears him from his thoughts. The sound of glass breaking and crashing to the floor, along with a solid thud, leads him to believe the home is under some sort of attack.

The sketchbooks falls to the floor as he speeds into the kitchen to investigate. He stops after he surveys for an intruder, but only sees the broken kitchen window and a large red brick laying among the shattered pieces of glass on the floor.

Eric bounds down the stairs.

"What the hell was that?" he yells.

"It is okay," Eli says, bending over to pick up the brick. It has a note strapped to it with a rubber band. "Someone just sent a note through the window."

Breathing heavy, Eric walks to the window and peers outside into the darkness. He hears the distant sounds of traffic and a dog barking. He turns back to Eli, who is looking at him with a concerned expression.

"What is it?" Eric asks.

Eli holds the note out for him. "It is for you," he says.

Eric takes it from him and reads it out loud. "We know what you did, Eric Wayne," he reads. His chest tightens and anxiety consumes him.

Eli waits patiently for an explanation, but Eric is disinclined to offer one.

Eric glances at him. "Yeah, I guess it was for me." He turns and looks at the window. "Sorry about the window, I'll get it fixed for you."

"No need," Eli says casually. "The board is responsible for maintenance. I will inform them we had an incident."

Eric's face flushes and he walks past Eli. "I'll be upstairs, if you need me," he says quietly.

Before Eric reaches the stairs, Eli calls to him. "Is it safe for me to assume this is linked to the incident that landed you as a sober companion?" He turns, hoping for an explanation.

Eric glances over his shoulder at him and starts walking up the stairs. "Yes."

Eli trails him but only to the bottom of the stairs.

"Your secret is safe with me, whatever it is. I would not tell the board on you," Eli says.

Eric stands at the top, considering the vampire's invitation to share his horrible transgression.

"I appreciate that. But you may not feel that way if you knew what it was."

Eli contemplates what his sober companion could possibly have done to have him so twisted up inside. He can think of nothing that would change his opinion of him. There is no transgression that he himself hasn't already committed, and his capacity for compassion and forgiveness of others is nearly boundless because of it.

Chapter Seven

For the entirety of the next morning and afternoon, Eli continues his research in the study. He compiles a list of books on witchcraft he thinks could possibly help him with the curse and emails the list to Nathan and Diane, who reply to him within minutes saying they'll get right to work searching for them.

Later in the evening, Eric joins him in the study and does his own reading.

"Still reading law books?" Eli comments, looking up from his laptop.

"Yeah. Just in case I decide to get back into it someday."

"Could you legally? Or did the incident ruin that for you?" Eli hopes that by encouraging Eric to talk about, or around, the subject, he will eventually drop his guard and tell him his big secret.

"Technically, after my sentence is over, I would be allowed back into law school."

"And when is it over?"

Eric peers up from his book and sees Eli's intrigued expression. He rolls his eyes and ignores the question.

"Fine," Eli says. "I'll get it out of you yet."

Eli's phone rings and they both jump. He pats the stacks of

papers on his desk and finally discovers the phone buried under one.

"Why don't you keep your phone where it's easy to access? You always have to fish around for it," Eric grumps.

"To be honest, I do not really care for these things. They kind of annoy me," Eli says. "Hello?"

Eric watches Eli's face turn somber.

"I see. Yes, Captain. I will be right there," he says and hangs up the phone.

Eric closes his book. "Do we have a case?" he asks.

"I'm afraid so," Eli says quietly.

Noticing his hesitation, Eric senses something is wrong. "Well? Do we need to get going?"

"Yes, of course," Eli says. He shoves the phone in his pocket and grabs his coat from the coat rack.

"Wait, did you eat yet?" Eric says, putting his own coat on.

"No, but there's no time now. We need to go."

"What's the rush?"

"I do not know for sure, but the Captain wants me there right now."

In less than twenty minutes they arrive at a storage unit facility by the water on the lower east side of Manhattan. They are once again met by a somber scene with yellow police tape, an unusually large number of police cars all running their red and blue lights, and a surly Captain Meyers impatient for the vampire sleuth to arrive.

"Believe it or not, I am actually glad to see you this evening, vampire," Captain Meyers says to Eli.

"What has happened, Captain?" Eli asks.

Without answering, Captain Meyers signals for them to follow as he leads them past a long block of storage units to the end of the row where three units have their doors open. A hushed group of nearly a dozen police officers and crime scene evidence technicians hover just outside of the doors and peer inside. The Captain orders the group to make room for him to get through. Eli and Eric wade through the group, peering around heads and shoulders but unable to see until they stand just inside the unit.

Eric feels the life drain out of him as he lays eyes on the most gruesome scene imaginable. Ten human bodies, hanged by their necks, dangle from short chains affixed to the ceiling of the storage unit. Each body has been gored to death. Blood still drips from the exposed entrails. Beneath the bodies the cement floor is flooded with a dark puddle of blood.

"There are three units like this," Captain Meyers mutters, shaking his head. "Thirty people. Dead."

The bodies sway and gently knock into each other like hanging cattle carcasses in a meat factory. On the unit's back wall, Eli spots large letters.

"What is the writing on the wall?" He asks.

The Captain nods him towards it. "Take a look."

Eric glances at the floor and throws his arm in front of Eli. "Wait. What about the blood?"

"He won't hurt anything walking through that," Captain Meyers says. We've already done a preliminary sweep. You may want to put these on, though," he says, handing him a pair of protective crime scene slippers to keep his shoes dry.

Eric leans down and whispers to Eli as he slips them over his shoes.

"The blood looks fresh, Eli. Don't do this if you think it's going to threaten your sobriety!"

Eli regards him with an equally concerned look, and stares at the back wall. "I know. But I need to see what it says."

Reluctantly, Eric watches as Eli does his best to navigate the hanging maze of bodies without touching them. He disappears behind the bodies.

At the back wall, Eli reads the blood words and for the first time in centuries, he feels fear.

Eric holds his breath until Eli emerges from the abhorrent display of carnage. He didn't know it was possible for Eli to appear any paler, but all hint of color has drained from him.

An evidence technician approaches Eli and offers to take the bloody slippers from his feet. Eli accepts the help and mechanically lifts each foot as the technician removes them with gloved hands.

Captain Meyers lights up a cigar and takes an unusually deep puff on it.

"Any ideas, Mr. Alexander?" He says.

"No," Eli says, his voice hollow.

"You'll do the blood remnant test?" Captain Meyers says.

Eli nods. "Yes, of course. Can I get some gloves?"

Eric watches as Eli robotically puts on the gloves and steps in just far enough to swab a drop of blood from the closest hanging body. With the sample on the gloves, Eli walks out of the unit and away from the law enforcement crowd to test the blood.

Following him, Eric is unnerved by Eli's sudden frigidity.

"You okay?" He calls.

Eli stands in a darkened spot a good distance from the crime scene, facing away. Reluctantly, he dabs the blood on his tongue and waits for the remnant memories to hit. This blood still has some live cells. It immediately piques his hunger.

Because the murders are so fresh, the memories and the emotions hit Eli's mind so hard and fast that a sharp pain shoots through his head. He groans and plows his face into his hands in an attempt to stop the pain threatening to shoot out of his eyes like lightening.

"Eli! What's wrong?" Eric calls, running up to him.

Eli continues to groan and squeeze his face and head as the blood remnants and his hunger consume him. He grimaces, unable to prevent Eric from seeing that his fangs have come out.

"Oh, damn it," Eric says, looking around to be sure none of the law enforcement officers are watching Eli nearly slip into a relapse. Luckily, their attention remains on the carnage within the storage units. "Eli! What's going on? Is it the blood? I knew I should have made you eat before we came."

"Just give me a minute," Eli replies. "I just need … I just need a minute." He stumbles away and rounds a corner into another row of storage units, backing into the metal door of one and resting against it.

Eric follows him and is relieved to be out of the line sight of witnesses. Angry and distressed about a potential relapse, he paces nervously in front of Eli waiting for whatever is wrong with him to pass.

"God, no," Eli says, exacerbated.

As was repeatedly drilled into him during his sober companion training, Eric calms his demeanor so that his tranquility will transfer into Eli.

"Eli," he says quietly. He puts his hand on Eli's shoulder to calm him. "Tell me what's going on."

"This is not good, Eric," Eli says finally. The remnants begin to dissipate and the pain in his head relents. "This is really bad."

"What did the writing on the wall say?"

"Elias Alexander, this is for you," he says.

Eric balks. "That's … what it said? You mean, whomever did this is trying to get to you?"

Eli nods and sinks back against the metal storage unit door. Considering Eli always carries himself with proper posture and an energetic confidence, seeing him slump despondently into the wall has Eric nearly as unnerved as the hanging bodies.

"Okay," Eric says. "Did you see who did it, from the blood sample?"

Eli nods grimly.

"Great! I'll get the Captain, you can tell him and we can get outta here," Eric says.

He begins walking around the corner but Eli darts to him, grabs his arm and pulls him back.

"What's wrong?"

"The Captain cannot know who did this," Eli warns.

"What? Why not? He's going to ask you what you saw!"

"I know. But he cannot know. If he finds out, we'll be at war by tomorrow."

"War? Oh, my god," Eric says. "Well who did this?"

Eli hears the Captain approaching before Eric. He nods his head, silently warning Eric not to say anything. He steps around the corner and meets the Captain as he walks.

"Well? Who did this?" Captain Meyers demands.

"Captain, these people did not see who killed them. They were blindfolded. Someone knows I am on this end of things, and that is why they left the note in blood. They took great care to be sure the blood remnant test would not work. Whomever slaughtered the humans wanted them to be found right away. My guess is in an effort to exploit me somehow. Perhaps to derail my sobriety."

"Do you have any idea who it could be? Are we looking for humans, or for vampires?"

"The difficulty is, Captain, there is strong motive on both sides to lash out at me. I will do some investigating in the vampire community. I'm afraid that's the best I can offer for now," he says.

"Humph," the Captain groans. "All right, Alexander. Let me know what you find out. You can go now."

"Captain," Eli says as the Captain begins walking back to the carnage.

"Yeah?"

"I am very sorry for the loss of life that occurred this night. I will do everything in my power to bring the perpetrators to justice. You have my word," Eli says.

The Captain nods. "See that you do. If you are in any way connected to these human deaths, I'll stake you myself." He lets out a steady puff of smoke before returning to the horrific scene.

Eric examines Eli's face and is relieved to see his fangs have retracted. "Ready to get out of here?"

"Yes, we must go." Eli says.

Once clear of the scene, Eric sighs. "So, the blood bothered you?"

"No, it was fine," Eli says.

"Don't lie. Come on, it's okay. You didn't relapse. It was dead blood, right?"

"It was very *fresh* dead blood," Eli corrects. "It still had some live cells."

"So it did stir your hunger?"

"Yes, a little."

"You overcame it, Eli. That was a big temptation and you handled it very well. You should be proud of yourself!"

"Proud?" He snorts. "I'm not proud of anything that happened back there."

"A lot happened back there," Eric says. "But my job is to monitor your sobriety, and in the face of a lot of partially fresh blood, you didn't flip out. You did great."

"Just out of curiosity, will that show up on a blood test?"

"We'll run a test when we get back, just to see," Eric says. "You're not worried about being accused of relapse though, right?"

"No. That is not what worries me."

"Good. So, what did you see? Who killed those people?"

"Vampires, Eric. Vampires are responsible."

"Oh my God," Eric breathes. "No wonder you couldn't tell the Captain. You're right, it would have started a war right away."

"The peace established between humans and vampires would erode instantly. It would be a nightmare, for everyone. The Human-Vampire War, all over again."

Eric considers the enormity of the situation as they walk the streets in silence. The most violent and brutal parts of the war happened before he was born, and he cannot imagine having to go through such horrific battle in this modern era.

"Do you know them?" Eric asks.

"Know who?"

"The vampires that did this. Do you know -"

"Yes, Eric. I know who did this." Eli stops walking and pulls Eric to the side to allow other pedestrians to pass by them. "But do not ask me anything further, it will only endanger you."

"All right," Eric says reluctantly. "Just tell me this: are you in danger now? Are they coming after you?"

They begin walking again.

"That is a definite certainty."

"What are you going to do?"

"Nothing."

"What?" Eric stumbles over the curb as they come to a new sidewalk. "What do you mean, nothing?"

"Until I know who is ultimately responsible for this, there is nothing I can do."

"But you saw who did it, right? Through the blood remnant test?"

"Yes. But a blatant act of violence of this capacity most certainly came from an order from somewhere higher up in the vampire chain of command. I must identify the commander."

"Makes sense," Eric says. "How can I help?"

Eli laughs. "I do not expect you to get remotely involved with any of this, Eric. This is vampire business."

"The threat of a second Human-Vampire War could very well become my business. I have a vested interested in maintaining peace between us."

"That does not mean it is a good idea for you to get involved," Eli chides.

"Who are you, my father?" Eric retorts.

Eli stops and turns to him, trying to hide his amusement. "What?"

"You think just because you're this famous centuries-old vampire, and I'm just a lowly human, that you have a right to be concerned about vampire affairs but I don't?" Eric throws his hands out in frustration.

"Where is this coming from? I do not think you're a *lowly* human!"

Eric grumbles. "Eli. We just saw bodies hanging from the

ceiling of storage units," he says. "Human beings murdered by vampires and hanged up like ... like sides of beef!" He runs his hands through his hair. "And you know who did it, and if it gets out, the sanctity of our existence will instantly erode. For God's sake, I can't just sit by and do nothing! Let me help you stop this nuclear event from happening!"

Eli feels himself opening up to the idea of letting Eric in on this. He understands Eric's struggle to cope with the situation, his anxiety evident as he repeatedly runs his hand through his hair and paces in a small circle on the sidewalk. Eli is briefly overtaken by an old memory of Elizabeth displaying the same signs as she struggled to accept Eli's claim that vampires were real, and he was one of them.

"This scares you," Eli says softly.

Eric plants himself directly in front of him. "More than anything," he says. "Lives are at stake."

"You worry about human lives."

"*All* lives, Eli. This isn't an *us versus them* thing, or *you versus me*," he says with a shrug. "This is about peace among species. It's about being able to co-exist. What other cause could be more worth fighting for?"

"I could name one," Eli says, turning and beginning to walk again.

Eric catches up with him. "You're not seriously blowing me off right now, are you?"

Eli maintains his reserved demeanor, but smiles. "No, Eric. I am not."

"So what could possibly be more important to you than stopping the breakdown of our entire society?"

Eli grins, certain nothing could ever be more important than his entire life's pursuit of Elizabeth. He glances at Eric, chuckling at his disgruntled expression. "What, indeed."

On the subway, Eric sits on the plastic orange seat while Eli leans against the silver stability pole silently ruminating over the night's new developments. The blood remnant test clearly showed him the faces of vampires responsible for the murders. Moreover, they are members of the Boston bloodline that he turned in to the authorities in exchange for his asylum.

He gazes at Eric, who sits silently staring at the grimy train floor. Bringing him in on this could seriously endanger his life. But for the first time in eons, Eli's mind is clearer and focused, more than usual. After not having seen Elizabeth in so long, but now having Eric as a constant companion, Eli feels relaxed and … fulfilled?

"Seriously?" Eli blurts out loud, ready to argue with himself about his suspicious feelings of contentment.

Eric looks at him and raises an eyebrow. "Who are you talking to?"

Eli shakes his head and takes a seat by Eric. He leans in, taking care not to let anyone overhear them.

"The vampires responsible for this seek retaliation against me, for what I did to their kin in Boston," he says in a hushed voice.

Eric nods and listens with a pained expression.

"No human can know about this. If we are to pursue this, I need you to be clear on that."

"No, they cannot. I understand that," Eric says.

"The Boston bloodline runs deep. The members that I am personally responsible for their capture by the authorities have been put to death for their crimes."

"I see," Eric says. "And that's why the family is after you."

"Yes, but vampire sects do not work like the human mafia or anything. They are not just going to hunt me down and kill me. That would be too easy. They have been looking for an excuse to revolt since the War ended. They will use me as a catalyst to start it, and when it does, they'll turn their attention away from me and focus it on destroying the human institutions."

"So are you saying you're not in danger, but humans are?"

"I am a member of the original vampire bloodline, which is sacred. My age and my lineage protect me against assassination. I am the son of one of the three original vampires. But that does not mean they will not destroy my life, and the lives of anyone in my life."

"So what are you saying?"

"I am saying, Eric, they are going to come at me hard and fast, and it is you I worry about getting hurt."

"Eli, I'll do anything to stop this from happening. We can't afford another War. Don't worry about me. Worry about that!"

Eli smiles. "You seem so undaunted by these circumstances. You are not dissuaded by many things then?"

"Not when it's the right thing to do," Eric says. "The right thing is always worth fighting for."

"The valiant Eric Wayne," Eli says. He leans back and pats him fondly on the back. "A true savior of the people."

"I don't know about all that," Eric says, rubbing his face. "This world we live in is maddening. There is so much potential for advancement in life, in science, health, even space exploration. All we have to do is stop fighting each other and start working towards the same goals. Imagine the progress we could make if we weren't battling each other for power and control."

"Space exploration, huh?" Eli says, playfully elbowing Eric in the ribs in an attempt to lighten his mood.

"You jest, but if things like *you* exist here on earth, imagine what might be crawling around out there in the universe!"

Eli laughs. "The way you see the world is truly remarkable, Eric."

"The way we see anything is all we really have," Eric says.

"Now you sound like the thousand year-old here," Eli says with a smirk. "I am supposed to be the wise one."

The subway train reaches their final stop and they depart the empty car.

"Think about it," Eric says. He pulls his coat tight to seal out the cold night air. "Everyone experiences life so differently, and it's literally all in our minds."

"Yes, and the mind can be just as dangerous as the real world," Eli says.

"An un-manicured mind, yes."

"Un-manicured?"

"Yeah. If you let bad thoughts and attitudes grow like weeds in your mind, everything in life will be a bad experience. You'll always be saying, *why me?* Life will feel like a cruel test, one you're doomed to fail. But, if you make it a point to guard your thoughts against negativity, pull out the weeds, and stay positive no matter what, life is an adventure!"

"My friend, you have a refreshing perspective on things," Eli says. "That explains your eternal idealism."

"Have you ever read Viktor Frankl's *Man's Search for Meaning?*"

"Read it? I published it," Eli says.

Eric stares at him wide-eyed. "What do you mean, you published it? You knew him?"

Eli nods. "I was a Captain in the U.S. Army in World War II. I helped with the liberation of concentration camps in Europe. That is where I met him. Mr. Frankl was an extraordinary man. Not only did I get to read his work, but I felt moved to facilitate the translation, printing, and distribution of it."

"Did he know what you are?"

"Not at that time, but years later, shortly after the Human-Vampire War started, I visited him. There were a select few humans that I wanted to come forward to, so they could know my truth."

Eric smacks him on the arm with gusto. "Seriously? What did he say? Was he totally wigged out by it?"

"No! In fact, with a very straight face, he told me that I could expect to be persecuted for my ... uniqueness, but to take heart and remember that the pendulum always returns to positivity. To the side of all that is just and good in life. He said as long as I always choose goodness and love, no manner of oppression can take my soul. "

"That's incredible!" Eric says, jumping in excitement. "Then you totally get it! You understand what he said. Life is all about the meaning we assign to it, yes?"

Eli nods and they stop at the bottom of the cement steps to their townhouse, their conversation carrying them all the way home.

"Do you practice his method, in your own life?" Eric asks.

"I have maintained a positive outlook on life," Eli replies.

"You've been alive so long. Would you say optimism is the key to you flourishing?"

Eli considers if his optimism of being with Elizabeth is the same thing as having a positive outlook on life. Despite being a proactive member of society who throughout the centuries fought for equality and justice, his mind has always been focused on her.

"I'm sure the answer lies somewhere between optimism and love." Eli takes the keys out of his pocket to unlock the door.

"Oh, I get it," Eric says with a sly grin. "You're a romantic!"

"Hopeless."

They enter the dark townhouse and Eric flips on lights as he goes. He glances at his watch and scowls. "You better eat! Aren't you hungry?"

Eli hangs his coat and heads to the kitchen. "Starving."

"So, what's our first step in going after this Boston vampire faction?"

"I do not want to do anything until I get some backup."

"Backup?" Eric joins him at the kitchen table. "What kind of backup?"

"Backup in the form of my oldest friend in the world." He smiles wide.

"Wow, so you do have friends?"

Eli smirks. "Yes, Eric, of course I have friends."

"And you think he can help you?"

"He will help me and like it."

"Does your friend have a name?"

Eli pulls a cold pint of synthetic from the refrigerator and gulps it down. He wipes the thick red sludge from his mouth and wrinkles his nose.

"His name is Cicero."

Chapter Eight

Three days later in the early morning, a pounding knock at the front door jolts Eric from his slumber. He glances at his watch and groans at the time, rolling over and stuffing his pillow over his head. The pounding knock comes again, and he curses.

"Eli? Are you going to answer the door?" he calls to Eli, but gets no response. The knock comes a third time and he stumbles out of bed and down the stairs. He fumbles with the locks and finally opens the door, squinting as the sunlight accosts his sore eyes.

A short, wiry man with wide green eyes and reddish hair, and a look of shock on his face, stares at him with his mouth half open.

"Yes?" Eric says. He waits for an answer but the man just stands there, head cocked to the side, staring silently.

"Oh, hey!" Eli calls, jogging to the door from his study. "Sorry, I was lost in a good book." Lately, during every second of Eric's sleep, Eli barricades himself in the study to comb through his books in hopes he will find an answer to the curse.

The wiry man looks from Eli to Eric as if he is the one awaiting an explanation.

"Eric, this is my oldest friend in the world: Cicero," Eli says. "And Cicero, this is my sober companion, Eric."

"Nice to meet you," Eric says drowsily.

"Lovely to meet ye," Cicero says, purposely trying to smooth out his thick Scottish accent.

Already feeling like the third wheel, Eric excuses himself and heads upstairs to shower.

"Well?" Cicero says, hands on his hips.

"Well what?"

"Invite me in, ye daft bastard!"

"Oh, of course! Come in, Cicero," Eli says with a chuckle.

Cicero crosses the threshold into the townhouse, and the two exchange a hearty hug.

"Always so good to see you," Eli says. He leads him into the sitting room. "Do you want something to drink? I have synthetic, synthetic, or synthetic."

"Yech," Cicero says. "The mere thought of it makes me stomach lurch!"

"Tell me about it."

"You got any Scotch?" Cicero sits on the small leather love seat in front of the fireplace.

"But of course," Eli says. He pours the drink for both Cicero and himself and hands it to his friend, sinking down into the club chair opposite the love seat.

They both take a swig of the booze and fall into silence. Finally, Cicero sets his glass down on the end table.

"Okay, I see it," he says, nodding his head.

"I told you! Didn't I tell you?" Eli glances out towards the stairwell and listens, making sure the shower water is running upstairs so Eric doesn't hear their conversation.

"He's a spittin' image of her! What the hell did ye do?"

"I didn't *do* anything! I haven't seen Elizabeth in over fifty years, and about a month ago *he* shows up at my door as my sober companion!" He sits back.

Cicero nods his head. "Right, right. Does he know?"

"Know what? That he's a reincarnated version of my one true

love?" Eli snorts. "No, we haven't really had that conversation yet Cicero!"

"All right, calm doon. Are ye *sure* about him? I mean, does he have the mark and everything?"

"Yes! He has the mark, he looks identical to her, and he even *feels* like she did."

Cicero eyeballs him. "You didn't ... you know ..." he makes a sexual gesture that sets Eli off.

"What? No of course not!"

Cicero throws his hands up in surrender. "All right, calm doon ye paranoid bastard! I was just asking! Ye said he feels like her. What do ye expect me to ask?" He gulps down the rest of the Scotch, and Eli jumps up to refill it.

"I don't know what to do, Cicero. I haven't talked to him about it yet, and he's already twenty five."

"Ack, that's nae good," Cicero says, cringing. "You still can't find the witch? Nothing in the books?"

"Nothing," Eli says, dropping back into the chair.

"Ye know he's an addict, right?"

Eli's eyes jump from the floor to his friend. "What do you mean?"

"It's in his eyes. They're swollen and glassy. Way too red to be just fatigued. I've been hearin' about this a lot recently, ye know."

Eli shakes his head. "I'm sorry, addicted to what? What are you talking about?"

They both hear the shower water shut off upstairs, and they lean towards each other, hushing their voices.

"The sober companions. The humans that don't want vampires smellin' their blood. They get addicted to the chemicals and turn into druggies. Yer boy is an addict, Elias!"

Eli considers his friend's sincere expression and gazes past him towards the front door. Finally, he shakes his head. "No, I would be able to tell if he was."

"Ye cannot see it because yer too busy being in love with the boy," Cicero says.

"What? I'm not in love with ... Eric." The words feel like a lie as they leave his mouth.

"Uh-huh, sure," Cicero says, sipping the Scotch. "Ye have spent a thousand years loving yer precious Elizabeth. I've watched ye, remember? The look on yer face, the way yer actin' now, is nae different than when it was her." He points emphatically at his friend. "Yer souls are connected. Ye canna help it. Ye love the boy." Cicero watches as Eli squirms in silence. "I'd give him a go. He's pretteh."

"Cicero! You're not helping," Eli growls, groaning and covering his face.

Cicero chuckles. "Eli. Ye know I love ye. Yer my oldest friend. But ye got to stop this madness with Elizabeth. I'm afraid it's finally making ye flat crazy. I mean that, I'm very concerned for ye."

"I cannot give up now, I've been working on this too long."

"Ye haven't made nae progress in a thousand years! And she will never, ever agree to let ye turn her. Look where that leaves ye, Elias. Alone in the world! Always chasing something ye canna have. And it's killin' ye. I canna keep watching this happen to ye. It's disgustin' now. It's perverse."

"What if you were to help me look for the witch again?"

Cicero groans. "We tried that, remember? Nothing! There's no sign of that bitch! Everywhere a dead end! Why do ye want to go down that road again?"

"Cicero, I have no other options. Please. Eric is running out of time. If I find her soon, maybe I can save his life."

"You want to save his life? Turn him," Cicero says sternly. "Turn him. He'll let ye. Then ye'll have yer soul mate with ye for all time. So what if it's a boy? Yer lucky to even have one! I never have."

Eli slumps in his chair, staring helplessly at his oldest friend.

Cicero throws back the rest of the Scotch and sets the glass down hard on the end table, cursing beneath his breath. The sad-puppy look on Eli's face has always managed to win over his sentimental side.

"All right, ye God damn lunatic," Cicero says. "Listen. Word is, Castor is in town."

"Castor? In New York? I'll be damned," Eli says.

Eli's memory of Castor has always been bittersweet. As the vampire that turned him that fateful night of the witch's curse, Eli hates him more than any other. But the familial connection between a vampire and his maker is difficult to deny. Eli likens it to the American tradition of being obligated to show up at Thanksgiving dinner and spend time with an unsavory relative when one would rather be burned at the stake.

"I don't think it's wise to look for him, Elias. It's too dangerous!"

"What other choice do I have? Plus he might know who's behind this Boston thing. The bloodline is coming for me and I've got to do something to stop them. They're planning a second War, Cicero."

"Damn it, ye're just full of trouble these days, aren't ye?"

"I need your help, with Eric and with this Boston thing. With Castor. Come on, Cicero. The world might end if we don't do something!"

"I know, I know," Cicero grumbles. "I'll help ye find Castor. And I'll help you with this Elizabeth thing one last time. But if ye want my opinion, ye should turn the boy and be done with it."

"Be done with what?" Eric plods down the stairs, catching only the tail end of Cicero's sentence. The smell of freshly showered skin with a hint of musky deodorant mask the scent of the chemicals in Eric's blood.

"Um, Eric, Cicero and I have some catching up to do, but how about we all get together for dinner tonight?"

"You want me to let you go out on your own? It's not even been a month, Eli. Protocol says you can't go out alone until two months have passed."

Eli pouts emphatically. "Yeah, I know, but Cicero came a long way to see me, and it would be too dangerous for you to go where we need to go. Please, Eric? I'll skip the outing when the two month mark rolls around. Promise."

Eric glances at Cicero. "All right, but I need a word with your friend first."

"Fair enough," Eli says, jogging out of the room. "I'll just get my things."

Cicero straightens, anticipating the lecture.

Eric sits rigid in the club chair across from the Scottish vampire and stares him down. "Eli's sobriety is very important to me," he says. "If you do anything to jeopardize his progress, I will hold you accountable."

"Ye have nothing to worry about, lad," Cicero says. "I wouldn't dare throw him off the wagon."

"You realize his legal independence depends on this program, right?"

"Absolutely, lad."

"No live blood. In fact, no synthetic either, while you're out. You can drink alcohol in limited amounts, and if you so much as smell a drop of fresh blood anywhere, you will remove him from the situation, am I clear?"

Cicero grins. "Clear as mud, yer soberness," he jokes.

Eric's flat expression melts into a frown.

"Aye, boy," Cicero says, growing serious. "I love him too. We've been friends almost a thousand years. I won't let anything happen to him. And I won't let anyone hurt him. He deserves better than to be put through the ringer, ye catch me? He's a good vampire. But he's an even better man."

"Ready, Cicero?" Eli reenters wearing his coat and holding a book and his cell phone.

"Readeh for some decent Scotch," Cicero says, standing up. "Ye need to upgrade yer selection! Yer slippin'!"

"Catch you later, Eric," Eli says.

"Be ready for a blood test when I get back, Elias," Eric shouts as the vampires head out the door.

"Yep!" Eli shouts back, closing the door behind him.

"Ach, ye see? Ye've already got ya a proper wife, Elias!"

Cicero erupts in guttural laughter and smacks Eli hard in the back as they head out in search of Castor.

"I want to avoid large groups of humans, so let's stick to the streets," Eli says.

"Are we going where I think we're going?"

Eli glances at his friend's face, now hardened with concern.

"Do you know of a better place to start?"

"No, lad," Cicero says. "I just never thought I'd be goin' back to the Maverick."

"We don't have time to waste, we have to go to the source. Besides, the Maverick isn't so bad. I support their general principles, it's their methods that can be a bit …"

"Perilous? Mutinous?"

"Well, there's that," Eli says.

"What if someone from Boston is there and sees ye? They'll wallop you on sight!"

"They already know I'm here, Cicero. They've made that clear with the note written in blood at the scene of the storage unit murders. Plus Jeremiah already paid me a nice little visit."

"Ach! Jeremiah, that bastard! I never could stand the sight of that rat!"

"And in the midst of this, Cicero, Eric saw everything. Jeremiah, the murders. I told him I know who is behind this. I have totally roped him in and he wants to help me stop these guys."

Cicero stops walking long enough to smack Eli on the back of the head.

"Hey! What was that for?" Eli complains.

"What the hell are ye thinkin'? The more ye tell him, the more danger he's in. Don't ye use your head anymore, Elias?"

"I know, Cicero! I tried explaining that to him, but he is adamant about preventing another War."

Cicero scowls.

"I won't let anything happen to him," Eli says, trying to convince both Cicero and himself that he can keep Eric safe.

Cicero wags a finger in his face. "Of course ye'll try, but have ye forgotten that yer not even close to being at yer full capacity of strength?"

"No of course not," Eli says sheepishly. "Jeremiah nearly whipped me." Eli kicks at a rogue stone on the sidewalk.

"If Jeremiah can whip ye, think of what the Boston family could do! Yer not safe either, my friend. Are ye seriously going to stay on this rehab thing? Drinkin' that God-awful synthetic?"

"I have to, it's part of my asylum deal."

"Ach," Cicero groans. "What the hell happened to us, Elias? Either we have to let the humans starve us into pathetic little weaklings, or we have to qualify for a Vampire Visa and show it anytime we go out in public. I mean seriously! Why do we need Visas in our own countries? Granted, it's not this bad in Scotland, but ye'd think America was being run by the Nazis!"

"They're scared, Cicero," Eli says calmly.

"Scared? What's to be scared of? We're nae that different from them! So what if we eat different things. So do cows. Are humans scared of cows because they eat grass? No! What the hell!"

"Cicero, we are exponentially stronger than humans when we're on our natural food source. And given that some vampires have abused their power, it is no wonder the humans do everything they can to keep us restrained."

"I know there's the whole *bad apple* thing, but Christ! Hitler was a bad apple, but ye don't see the world's police punishing the Germans for his crimes!"

Eli laughs. "I am not arguing with you about the fairness of our station, Cicero. But we need to understand where the humans are coming from if we ever hope to renegotiate the terms of our freedom."

"My God ye're just so diplomatic, aren't ye? Did you ever think that maybe a second Human-Vampire War could do us some good? I mean, what if we won the second one? We could eliminate all this oppression!"

"We do not have to resort to violence to win our freedom, Cicero."

"Hah!" Cicero socks Eli in the arm. "Ye see that? Ye are a politician."

"No, I am not."

"Ye are! At least, you think like one, all diplomatic and peaceable. Ye're the people's politician. Ye should do something with yer talents, Elias, instead of spending yer days researching witchcraft."

Eli frowns. "You think I am wasting my time researching?"

"It's not that yer wasting time, Elias. It's that ye don't want to see the truth."

"What truth?"

"Witch's curse or nae, Elizabeth will always slip out of yer fingers. It's her fate. Haven't ye learned that, in a thousand years, Elias! Haven't ye learned that yet?"

"I still hold hope -"

"Ye'll hope for the rest of yer days, Elias. Ye'll hope, and ye'll be alone for it. Unless ye open yer eyes. Ye've got a chance to end this torturous cycle, with Eric."

"I like Eric, Cicero, but what about seeing Elizabeth again?"

"They're the same thing, Elias. Open yer eyes."

Eli and Cicero approach the entrance to the Maverick. The neon sign above the gold door glows bright pinkish-maroon against the dark night sky. Eli gazes up past the sign to the vampire guards barely visible on the four story rooftop.

A tidy, quiet line of humans and vampires dressed in ballroom dance attire begins at the gold door and extends around the building's corner. Eli and Cicero ignore their stares as they approach the seven foot vampire bouncer at the door. He scowls upon seeing the line jumpers approach.

"Can I help you?" the vampire bouncer says in an unearthly

deep voice.

"We're here to see the owner," Eli says.

"Do you have an appointment?" The bouncer flips pages on his clipboard.

"I do not need an appointment, my friend. I am Elias Alexander."

The vampire bouncer's eyes widen at the drop of the name. Whispers begin at the beginning of the line and quickly spread to its tail as humans and vampires share their amazement of seeing the celebrity vampire in person.

The bouncer pushes a button on his ear piece to communicate with the staff inside. "Please tell the owner Elias Alexander is here to see him." He gives Eli and Cicero a courteous bow and opens the door for them. "Mr. Alexander, I am pleased to meet you. Please enter."

"Good man," Cicero says, craning his neck to meet the bouncer's eyes as he enters ahead of Eli. He pats the bouncer's enormous bicep as he walks by, his eyes widening when he feels the steely strength beneath the long black shirt.

"Thank you," Eli says. He glances at the starry-eyed faces staring at him in the line and smiles.

The ambiance at the Maverick is regal and sophisticated. Despite being a nightclub by design, it has the feel of a royal ballroom mixer put on for top socialites. Waiters in tuxedos serve drinks to guests, their trays holding a mix of alcoholic and synthetic blood drinks. Vampire and human couples slow dance to 1930's music on the large rectangular dance floor while others chat quietly at standing tables spread throughout the club. Eli and Cicero make their way to the bar.

"What'll it be, darlings?" The bartender, a beautiful human in her early forties with bleached blonde hair styled in a short pixie cut and heavy makeup greets them with a wink.

"Ma'am," Eli says. "I am here to see the owner. My name is - "

"Elias Alexander!" A voice from behind him finishes his sentence.

Eli and Cicero turn to see the familiar smiling face of a vampire man turned in his 50's. Because most vampires are turned as younger humans, this one radiates more wisdom than even the oldest members of the race. His salt and pepper colored hair and slightly aged face, combined with an easy-going and down to earth personality, enable him to successfully network with humans and vampires.

"Frank," Eli says, returning the vampire's warm welcome hug.

Frank moves to Cicero, who begrudgingly returns the affectionate vampire's embrace.

"Good to see you both! It's been an age!"

"It has been a long time, Frank," Eli says.

Frank signals for the bartender to come back to their side of the counter.

"Dorothy, I want these two fine gentlemen to try our house drink. Would you be a dear and fix them some?"

"Of course, darling," Dorothy replies, flashing a sultry smile.

"That is really not necessary, Frank," Eli says. "We do not mean to impose. We simply need to speak with you about a rather urgent matter."

Frank lays a large palm on Eli's shoulder. "Elias, you always were a no-nonsense gentlemen. But honestly, what is life if you cannot take time to enjoy a drink with an old friend?"

"Gentlemen," Dorothy says as she places two wine glasses with a bright red drink mix on the counter. "Please enjoy."

"Thank you, love," Cicero says, gaze lingering on the bartender's fine features. "So, have ye worked here long?"

"Cicero," Eli chides. "Remember we are here on business." He grins at his friend.

Cicero corrects his posture, having begun to lean against the bar to get closer to Dorothy.

"Yes, yes, of course," he says, clearing his throat. He grins wide as Dorothy winks at him and walks away to tend to other customers. He takes a sip of the bright red drink and raises his eyebrows as he swallows. "Oh, my! This is bloody good! What is it?"

"Thank you, Cicero! It is my own creation. It has a base that is chemically identical to synthetic blood. Then, I added a special secret ingredient along with a mix of two fine red and white wines, and a splash of cranberry for additional flavor."

"Eli, ye've *got* to try this!" Cicero says, downing the rest of the drink from his glass.

Eli raises the glass to his mouth and breathes in the aroma, then takes a cautious sip. The taste is a pleasing mix of sweetness and wine without the usual intolerable bitterness of the synthetic.

"This is incredible!" Eli exclaims. He looks between Frank and Cicero, shocked by the sensation of consuming synthetic blood without feeling the need to gag. "Frank, you should put a patent on this and get it to the market. This could change the entire vampire food supply."

"Eli, you know vampires are not allowed to own or produce anything," Frank scolds.

"But ye own this club, don't ye?" Cicero says, licking the rim of his wine glass for remnants of the delicious drink.

"Technically, Frank Green, human from Vermont, owns this facility," Frank says with a wink. "It takes enough effort to keep the lid on my transgression here. I cannot imagine what an undertaking it would be to hide the true race of the owner of a nationwide chain of vampire beverages."

Cicero glares at Eli. "See this, Eli? See what ye could be workin' on right now? Fightin' for our right to a legal food source that doesn't taste like shite?"

Eli returns his glare but ignores him. He turns his attention to the urgency at hand.

"Frank, is there somewhere we can talk in private? It is important."

"Yes, of course," Frank says. "Come with me."

Cicero places his empty wine glass on the bar's counter and pouts. Seeing his friend's reluctance to leave Dorothy and her delicious nectar, Eli hands him his glass which he gladly accepts and chugs.

Eli and Cicero follow their sunny host through a door guarded by another large vampire through a long hallway that leads to Frank's cozy office. He sits at his large mahogany desk and gestures for his guests to sit in the overstuffed chairs in front of it.

Cicero looks around, admiring the elegantly designed office.

"I've got to say, Frankie, ye've got quite an establishment here."

"Thank you, Cicero," Frank says humbly. "I try." He claps his hands together and leans his elbows on his desk. "So, Elias, I am going to guess and say you are here with questions about Boston?"

"Is it that obvious?" Eli says.

"It's difficult to keep matters concerning the great Elias Alexander a secret," Frank says. The smile fades from his face, his mouth sliding into a frown. "They have found you and they mean business."

Eli nods. "Yes. Frank, I need you to tell me anything you know. I believe the Boston bloodline is planning a second war. I cannot let that happen, but I need to know their plans."

Frank sighs heavily and leans back in his captain's chair. He crosses his hands behind his head and carefully chooses his words.

"You understand the position this puts me in, Elias," he begins.

"I know, Frank. I truly do not wish for you to get involved. But you are his brother. There is no one else I could turn to that is privy to your information."

"There is a reason I am in New York and not Boston anymore, Elias. I do not agree with my brother's position on humans. He is the vampire equivalent of a human bigot. He has no respect for humans and no desire for equality. He simply wants to crush and conquer."

"I know this, Frank. That is why I did not find it difficult to turn in his top associates. It was a matter of cleaning up the streets, in my opinion."

"Yes!" Frank says, throwing his hands out. "And I was thrilled by your boldness, Elias! Finally, someone stood up to the bully that is Orlando Green! I cannot tell you how satisfying that was. I am just regretful that he is now out to burn you to the ground."

"Tell me, Frank. Please. What do you know?"

"Eli, if you want my advice, you should leave town. In fact, leave the country if you can."

"Why? I am not afraid of your brother," Eli says.

"Because, Elias, events are already unfolding behind the scenes that are guaranteed to at the very least tip the scales of power into the hands of vampires, and not the ones that want equality, like you and I would."

"You're saying a second war is inevitable?" Cicero says.

"The vampires behind this, my brother included, cannot seem to reach an agreement on whether or not to inflict a full blown war. There is conflict even among the different factions. If my brother has his way, then yes, the second war will happen. But another ... bloodline ... wishes for a more subtle, surgical takeover. More political, I could say."

"What bloodline do you speak of? Who else is involved?" Eli asks.

Frank looks at him coldly. "Yours, Elias. Yours."

Cicero looks at Eli, who maintains his gaze on Frank.

"What's he talkin' about, Eli?" Cicero asks.

"Is it my father?" Eli asks, eyes narrowing.

Frank's conflicted expression is but a glimpse of the harried relationship he has with his tyrannical brother.

"Frank, is it my father?" Eli presses.

"Orlando is still my brother, Elias," Frank says with a hint of desperation. "I know he must be stopped, but I do not wish to see him put to death. If the human authorities find him and know his plans, he will be executed for heresy. I cannot live with that. Even though I despise him."

"I understand that, Frank. I truly do. Just tell me, please – is Castor working with your brother? Are they in this together?"

"I do not believe Castor would have a war, Elias."

"So it is him?" Cicero demands. "It's Castor?"

"I have already said too much, gentlemen," Frank says as he stands. "I cannot give you anything else. I am sorry."

Eli and Cicero stand. Eli extends his hand to Frank and reluctantly smiles. "I understand. You have been helpful, regardless."

"I may have left Boston, Elias. But I am not as courageous a man as you. I am still bound to him by strings I am yet unable to cut."

"Maybe not, lad, but ye've got to give yerself more credit than that," Cicero says. "Ye're nothing like yer brother. Ye're definitely the better man there."

"Thank you, Cicero. Always a pleasure. Now, if you will please excuse me, I must pedal my beverage to the vampire crowd."

"I have one favor to ask of you, Frank. I need you to put me in touch with my father," Eli says.

Frank raises his eyebrows. "You mean, you don't know how to contact Castor?"

"Not anymore. I have not seen him in a long time. Can you help?"

"Yes, of course. I will get you his contact information."

"Thank you," Eli says.

"Hey, Frankie. Yer drink is damn good, do ye have a name for it?" Cicero asks.

Frank smiles. "Yes. I call it Salvation."

"Frank, out of curiosity, if you could fully launch your product, would you?" Eli asks.

"In a heartbeat, Elias. It would be a dream come true."

Frank leads them back into the club and shakes their hands

again. Just before leaving, Cicero grips Frank's arm.

"By the way, that Dorothy is a lovely lass! Is she available, or
_"

"Cicero!" Eli chides. "Let the man and his lovely bartender
be."

Frank grins and waves at the two as they leave the club.

Late that night, after firing off multiple unfriendly text message warnings to Eli about getting home ASAP and to be prepared for a relapse test, Eric enters the bathroom and prepares for his nightly injection. Unaware that Eli and Cicero have returned, he loads the syringe and taps his vein, waiting for it to swell up before sticking it with the needle. He cringes just before each injection, anticipating the excruciating burn. He slowly depresses the clear chemical into his body and waits for the pain to begin.

The searing heat spreads through his veins and the unbearable agony ensues.

"I hear it only hurts like that when you take too much of it."

Startled by Eli's voice, Eric drops the syringe onto the bathroom floor and squeezes his arm, trying to distract himself from the pain.

"Eli," he says through gritted teeth. Even the muscles in his jaw seize with pain. He does not possess the energy necessary to pretend he is not in complete agony, so he allows the process to continue as usual. He doubles over and groans loudly as he grasps the edge of the sink for balance.

"How long have you been addicted, Eric?" Eli's face darkens.

"Eli, I can explain," Eric croaks. If both his health and Eli's sobriety weren't truly at risk now, Eric would think the situation funny.

"How long?" Eli demands.

"It's not what it looks like," Eric says, a wave of unbearable pain shooting through his head. Blood rolls out of one nostril and drips onto the floor.

Eli grabs him by the neck and drags him across the floor, pinning him against the wall. "Do not lie to me, Eric! How long have you been an addict?"

Eric squeezes his eyes closed, feeling that his head is about to explode. "Three years," he whispers, the pain knocking the strength from his voice.

Eli scowls in disapproval. "Three years? Can't you see what this is doing to you? You're about to have a stroke!"

"I tried … I tried to stop, but I can't."

Eli feels the warmth of the blood as it drips from Eric's nose onto the back of his wrist. It smells repulsively of chemicals. Eric's chin drops and Eli pushes it back up so he can examine his eyes, the whites of which are completely pink with dark red veins swelling inside them. Eric's body begins to seize and his eyes roll back in his head.

"Cicero!" Eli yells.

Cicero speeds up the stairs to answer his friend's call of desperation.

"Ach, bloody hell! He's OD'd!"

Eric falls unconscious and Eli catches him before he slumps to the floor. He picks him up and stares at his blotchy face. "What the hell do we do?"

"I don't know. But I can feel the heat off his skin from here, he's burnin' up. Throw him in the tub and chill him down!"

Eli rips back the shower curtain and carefully places Eric down in the bathtub. He turns on the cold water and closes the drain, the tub quickly filling with freezing water.

"What else? What else?" Eli yells in a panic.

"Ach, I don't know if it'll work or not, but I've heard it's like a histamine response. Do ye have a first aid kit anywhere? We'll shove some pills in him and see if that works!"

"Watch him!"

Eli runs down the stairs to the kitchen and retrieves the first aid kit, pulling out two packets of Benadryl. He tears them from their pouches and is back at Eric's side in five seconds. He squeezes Eric's jaws open and stuffs the pills down his throat. He feels Eric's jugular for a pulse. Agonizing seconds later, a weak pulse flutters beneath his fingertips.

"Pulse," Eli breathes. "He has a pulse."

Cicero covers his eyes with his hand and groans in relief. "Bloody hell that was a close one."

The blood from Eric's nose drips into the now half full tub, swirling around gently in the water. By the time Eric regains consciousness, the water is pink.

The faucet squeaks as Eli turns off the cold water. Eric is already shaking and is just opening his eyes. He sucks in a deep breath of air and coughs.

"What happened?" Eric moans. The pain has subsided from his body except for his head, which now hurts worse than any hangover he's ever had. He blinks to clear his vision and is horrified to see that he is lying in a tub of bloody cold water. He starts to get up but Eli pushes him back down.

"Take it slow," Eli says. "You were about to burst into flames. We need to make sure the fire is out before you get out of here."

Shaking and feeling completely wiped out, Eric also feels an impending sense of doom. "What is wrong with me? Is this from the medicine? I feel like I'm dying or something."

"You said you've been addicted for 3 years?"

"Yes," Eric says, teeth chattering. "From the beginning."

Eli and Cicero exchange a knowing look. "That's no coincidence," Cicero says. "I've told you before, Elias. I do not trust this system. It is corrupt."

"I ... I'm sorry," Eric says, trying to suppress the impending emotional meltdown that accompanies many cases of overdose. "I am supposed to help you stay sober, but I myself am an addict." Unable to control the tears streaming from his reddened eyes, he wipes angrily at them. "I'm a damn hypocrite."

Eli sighs. "No, you're not a hypocrite, Eric," he says. "Your addiction and mine are very different."

"I'm your sober companion, Eli. I am the very definition of a hypocrite!"

"We just need to get this stuff out of your system. Then you will be fine."

"The court won't let me do this without taking injections," Eric says. "They'll pull me from the job and I don't want to go to prison!"

Cicero's head turns. "And the plot thickens," he mumbles.

"Cicero, hush," Eli says. "Eric, what are you talking about?"

Eric leans his head back against the shower wall. "I wasn't supposed to tell you. The reason I've been assigned to this job was to avoid a prison sentence for … for killing a vampire."

"Here we go," Cicero mumbles.

"You killed a vampire? How did it happen?" Eli asks.

Eric sniffs and grimaces as he swallows a mouthful of blood draining from his sinuses down the back of his throat. "It was with Robin. She is a vampire rights attorney. One of her clients went through rehab but relapsed hard and attacked her on the street one night. She and I just had dinner and were coming out of the restaurant. I panicked. I didn't know what else to do, so I grabbed a weapon and stabbed him through the heart. There were tons of witnesses. A half dozen cell phone videos. They had my ass before his ashes even hit the ground."

"You were defending her, Eric. I would have done the same thing," Eli says.

"So they gave me a choice of prison or helping vampires with their rehabilitation."

"A generous offer," Cicero chimes in.

"Cicero, please!"

"Ach, come on! If it had been the other way around, it would have been instant death for the vampire. That's the way this world works, Eli. There's no use in denying it anymore. We are animals to them, nothing more."

"All right, Eric. I think it's safe to take you out of your blood bath," Eli says, helping Eric stand.

"I have to keep taking it, Eli," he says, water dripping noisily from his clothes into the bath. "I can't do this job without it. I'm screwed."

"What if you didn't need it?" Eli says.

Both Eric and Cicero laugh at the idea. "Seriously? You want the lad to hang around starving vampires smellin' like a juicy steak?" Cicero says.

"Not other vampires, per se," Elias says. "But I can handle it."

Eric looks for a sign Eli might be joking, but he is not.

"You're serious? It would ruin your sobriety! I would be responsible for you relapsing!"

"Eric, I walk past hundreds, maybe thousands of humans on the streets, and in the subways, most of them never having touched the chemicals. I smell their blood but you do not see me attacking anyone, right? I can handle having one human in my house. If we are careful about cuts and so forth, we will be fine."

"Careful? Careful until the boy cuts himself shaving? Then ye'll rip his throat out like a mad dog? Think about this, Elias! Careful doesn't always work," Cicero warns.

Eli pulls a towel off the rack and wraps it around Eric's soaking shoulders. "Let's get you to your room," he says, catching Eric as he nearly drops to the floor.

"Why do I feel so heavy?" Eric mumbles, struggling to hold his eyes open.

"You just had a major adrenaline rush and you're crashing. Sleep it off, you should be fine," Eli says.

With Eric asleep in his room, Eli and Cicero convene in front of the fireplace in the sitting room.

"Don't look at me like that," Eli says in anticipation of his friend's scrutiny.

"Elias. Listen to me. When are ye gonna open yer eyes? This whole sobriety thing is a farce. And given all the human addicts it's producin', I'd say someone has an ulterior motive."

"It would seem so," Eli says.

"Ye should cut and run from here. Come with me back to Scotland. It's nothing like this back home."

"This is my home, Cicero."

Cicero snorts. "Ye mean this is where ye think Elizabeth will show up, eh? In case ye didn't notice, yer soul mate is upstairs sleepin' off an overdose! Ye both need to get the hell out of here before the shite hits the fan. Humans," he says, angrily slumping down in the loveseat, "humans – especially Americans – always have an agenda. Whoever makes the most money and power wins the game of life. That's all they care about here. Mad capitalist bastards."

"Cicero. I'm not sure humans are behind this. Think about it: sober companions become hopeless addicts. The number of vampires in rehab has tripled over the last month. The demand for chemicals is skyrocketing. Human sober companions need it. Vampires on rehab need it. Imagine what would happen if the demand overruns the supply, or if the supply were to … end."

"Anarchy," Cicero mumbles. "A million hungry vampires relapsing at the same time. A million human sober companions falling ill from withdrawal from the chemicals, their addictions exposed and the humans that designed the system will be blamed for it."

"So the country would become one bloody massacre. The entire system would collapse and vampires and humans would call for a revolution. Whoever saw this coming will already have planned their ascent to power. It is vampires that stand to gain the most from this. Could this be what Frank was talking about?"

Cicero shrugs. "I don't know. What do we do about it?"

"We have no evidence, this is all just hearsay."

"Then you have two choices, Eli. You either make it your business, or you save yerself and get out."

"I am no politician, Cicero."

"Aye, but ye used to be a feared and respected leader. Ye can rise to power again! Take the reins and drive the vampires out of this autocratic nightmare!"

"What's the point anymore, Cicero?"

"The point of what? Of living?"

Angered, Cicero jumps up from the sofa and grabs Eli by the collar, hoisting him out of the chair.

"Now ye listen here. Ye've spent a thousand years pining over something ye cannot have. It's time for ye to pull yer head out of yer ass and join the livin'! Get back in the game. Find a purpose to life that doesn't include -"

"That doesn't include *her*," Eli says, jerking away from his friend. "You want me to give up on her, after all this time?"

Cicero sighs. "Elias. Yer the most powerful vampire there is, and I ain't sayin' that because I'm biased. Yer even more powerful than Castor. Do ye want to know why? It's not because of yer age. It's yer wisdom, yer compassion, yer vision. Ye make one hell of a leader. Ye could guarantee equal rights for vampires in this barbaric human world. No one else has yer level of diplomatic ability, and of mercy, to do this the right way."

Eli growls and strides to the fire. Cicero joins him and they both stare into the bright embers.

Cicero's voice softens. "Elizabeth doesn't want to be a vampire, Elias. She makes the same choice every time. It's not what she wants!"

"Then she does not want me. Is that what you are saying?"

"I think she loved ye as ye are, but she has the right to choose her own destiny. Even if you find the witch and get her to break the curse, if Elizabeth does come back as herself, she'll eventually grow old and die, and that'll be the end of yer soul mate. Forever."

"Cicero. Without someone to love, why exist? What is the

point of living so long?"

"Who says ye'll not have love? Ye have the chance to spend eternity with a soul that was made fer ye. Eric will let ye change him. I'm certain of it. Ye don't have to snog him, but ye'd be daft to let him from yer sight."

"This life is ludicrous, Cicero," Eli says, dropping his head.

"I'll not fight ye on that one, Elias. It's madness. That's why ye need to surround yerself with good friends. People that love ye who are willin' to share in the madness with ye. It makes the journey easier to stomach. Stop waitin' around and start livin' again for yer own sake."

"Why do you think Eric would say yes to the change?"

"There's a strength in him I never saw in Elizabeth. And a bit of … hunger."

Eli sighs, knowing his friend's advice is more credible than he wants to admit. Cicero is the only one in existence besides himself that knows Elizabeth almost as well as he does. There were only a handful of reincarnated versions of Elizabeth that Cicero wasn't around to see. But if he chooses to turn Eric, does that mean he gives up on Elizabeth? Or is Eric actually the better option?

Chapter Nine

The next morning, Eric rolls out of bed with a pounding headache. He struggles through a fast shower, the hot water momentarily easing the pain. After drying himself off and getting dressed, he rummages through the medicine cabinet and the nightstand by his bed but finds the chemical vials and the syringes are missing.

"Damn it!" he curses. He slams the top drawer of the nightstand closed and looks at his shaking hands. He notices his heart is racing and he's sweating despite the coolness of the room. "Elias!" He calls out and storms downstairs.

Eli is waiting for Eric at the kitchen table with two mugs of hot coffee. He sips on his.

"Where is the medicine?" Eric demands.

"Sit down, Eric," Eli says quietly.

Eric runs a shaky hand through his damp hair and sniffs. "I told you I have to keep taking it."

"I know, or you will go to prison," Eli says with a chuckle.

"This is funny to you? This is my life, Eli!"

"I know it is," Eli says. "Sit down. Have some coffee."

Eric's agitation increases by the minute. "Why do you

vampires pretend you like drinking stuff like coffee and alcohol? You can't really get anything out of it, right?"

"Nutrition, no. But even *we vampires* enjoy things with different tastes and temperatures sometimes."

"I want the medicine. Tell me where you put it, or I'll just call one of my coworkers and get it from them."

"Eric, listen to me. You almost died of an overdose last night." Eli stands as Eric begins to pace like a caged animal. "You're in withdrawal right now. I know it doesn't feel good but you need to get off the stuff!"

Eric groans, his pain and frustration unnaturally amplified by the chemical withdrawal. "The only thing I need is another injection, then I'll be fine." He shoots Eli a deadly glance, but Eli is unfazed.

"Fine. I know what I need to do."

He storms off and runs upstairs to retrieve his cell phone. Before he can dial out, Eli appears at his side and yanks the phone out of his hand.

"Give it back, Eli!"

"No!"

Eric pulls at his hair. "God damn it, give it to me! I'll get my injection no matter what. Don't think I won't!"

"There is no way in hell you are going back on that stuff. It is toxic!"

Eric swipes for the phone. "Give me the phone!" He growls. Infuriated by Eli's moves to evade his reach, he lunges at him in a blind rage and swings wildly at him, landing a hit on Eli's jaw.

Eli maintains his composure but bends Eric's swinging arm behind him and pushes him into the wall, holding them there.

"Eric, no one understands the pain of withdrawal more than I do," Eli says.

Eric grunts and pushes against him, but Eli slams him back into the wall.

"Stop it! Stop fighting me. You'll only hurt yourself."

"If you keep standing between me and this injection, I'll kill you!"

Eli laughs. "Yeah, I remember saying that many times during my rehab."

Eric draws up his knee and it lands hard in Eli's stomach. He coughs and doubles over, his grip momentarily slipping. Eric makes a mad dash into the hallway but is stopped short just at the top of the stairs. Eli grabs him by the collar and yanks him back. He throws him into the wall, lifting him by the neck until his feet barely touch the floor.

As a reflex to the physical assault, Eli's fangs are out and his beastly temper begins to flare.

"I don't want to hurt you, Eric, but you need to control yourself!" He growls through his fangs. He notices Eric struggling to breathe and he lowers him. As he does, he picks up the faintest scent of blood. He leans in to smell Eric's neck. "It's already wearing off," he says. "Good. It won't be long now. Until then," he says, wrenching Eric down the stairs. "I know exactly where to put you."

Eli pushes him to the door to the small cellar and opens it.

"No! I'm not going down there!" Eric yells, bracing himself in the doorway like a cat bracing all fours against an impending dunk in a bathtub.

"Yes, you are!" Eli flips on the light and shoves him down the cellar steps.

To Eric's horror, attached to the stone wall is a single thick metal cuff on a long clunky chain. Eli wrestles him over to the chain and clamps it onto his wrist.

"No, come on, no! Don't do this! Eli, don't you dare leave me down here!" Eric screams.

"It won't take long for the chemicals to leave your system, Eric. I can already smell your blood. But you are acting completely insane and until this withdrawal phase is over, this is for your own good!" He backs away to avoid Eric's wild attempts to hit him.

"Eli, God damn it!"

"I am sorry, Eric. It will be over soon," Eli says, retreating up the stairs. He closes and locks the cellar door. Eric's painful screams reminding him of his own agony going through blood rehab.

"Yer just gonna leave him doon there?" Cicero approaches him, having let himself in.

"It has to be done," Eli says.

"He'll be madder than a wet hen when ye let him out. Just warnin' ye!"

"Yes, I am sure of it," Eli says. "Is the meeting with Castor set?"

Cicero nods. "Aye. It's on for tonight. But I got a bad feelin' about it, Elias. I don't trust him. Never have."

"I know," Eli says with a heavy sigh. "But we have to start somewhere."

That night, Eli and Cicero await Castor at a table in a popular bar and grill at a tavern in Greenwich Village. The ambiance of the restaurant is calm and quaint with low lighting. Each table is decorated with a white tablecloth and a small tea light candle inside a small red vase. A healthy mix of tourists and native area residents sit at tables and the bar.

"I could go for some B positive right now," Cicero grumbles. "Or more of Frankie's Salvation. At least the Scotch here is good."

Eli smiles. "I've always admired your directness, Cicero."

The millennial friends tense up as they see Castor come in to the restaurant. As usual, Castor is the most well-dressed patron in the restaurant in a suit and tie and a long black overcoat. He spots them and heads straight to their table, a smile playing across his handsome face.

Eli and Cicero stand out of respect for the elder vampire, giving him a slight bow as he reaches the table.

"Elias and Cicero, it has been too long," Castor says.

"Castor," Eli says. "Please, sit."

The three vampires sit and Castor orders a drink from the attending waitress. Castor pulls off his black leather gloves and places them neatly on the table. His eyes fall upon Eli and his gaze is affectionate as he silently studies the face of his creation.

"Castor, I am grateful for the meeting tonight," Eli says.

"There was a time you addressed me as father," Castor says coldly.

"Yes. Forgive me. Father," Eli says, voice strained.

"How long has it been, Elias? Half a century? Longer?"

Eli smiles uneasily. "It has been too long."

Castor cocks his head to the side. "What do you need, Elias? You normally don't come to me unless you need something." He laughs. "I suppose that is the duty of a parent. To always be there for their children." He looks pointedly at Cicero, who buries his eyes in his Scotch.

"Moriah," Eli says. "Do you know where she is?"

Castor raises an eyebrow. "Moriah? Now there's a name I haven't heard in eons. What is your interest in her?"

"I think you know," Eli says.

"Still struggling with the curse, I see. Do you not believe it to be a lost cause by now?"

"Unlike you, Father, I am still quite capable of feeling love."

Castor grins. "Love. Love is an illusion, Elias. A fleeting human emotion. Blood. Loyalty. Family. Now those are truly worthy endeavors. But love? Love is the ruin of man."

"When did you lose your soul? Or did you ever have one?" Eli says.

"My time is valuable, Elias. Speak your mind or I walk now."

"What do you know of the sobriety program?" Eli says.

Castor sighs and relaxes back into the chair. "I know as much as anyone else. The humans believe it to be the best way to coexist with us. Why do you ask?"

"Do you believe it will work? I mean, long term?"

"The program is not without its … defects," Castor says. He takes a sip of his Vodka. "Is something wrong, Elias? I heard that you are in the program. How is your sobriety, as they call it?"

"My sobriety is progressing," Eli says flatly. "I look forward to reaching legal independence once I complete the program."

"Nonsense," Castor says with a snort. "Do you really expect me to believe that, Elias? Do you really think you can exist on synthetic blood for the rest of your existence?"

"Father, I asked you here because I believe there to be something wrong with the sobriety system."

"Now you are making sense!"

"This is not about living on the synthetic," Eli says. He leans in and lowers his voice. "I foresee the system being overloaded. Demand will soon outweigh the supply, and when that happens, I fear it could start another War."

"What is there to fear, my son? If the supply runs out, yes there will be consequences. But do you not believe that to be a natural progression of an intrinsically flawed system?"

"I agree that the system is flawed, Father, but the repercussions could be devastating. For vampires and for humans. If we can do something to avoid such a catastrophe, do you not think we should?"

"By warning the humans that if they do not make immediate modifications the result will be pure chaos?"

"Yes, precisely," Eli says.

Castor thinks quietly to himself for a moment. He finishes his drink and picks up his gloves. He leans in close to Eli.

"Elias, I only have one question. The chips will fall as they may. But whose side will you be on when they do?" He pulls back and stares into Eli's stormy dark eyes. "Tsk, tsk, Elias. You always were so conflicted by your human morals. Perhaps it is time for you to advance your status and lead us into a new revolution?"

Cicero looks up from his drink and exchanges a concerned look with his friend. While uncertain about Castor's motives, Cicero wants nothing more than for Eli to lead the vampires to true freedom and equality. But at what cost?

"You would have me start a war, Father?" Eli whispers.

Castor chuckles. "No, Elias. I would have you end it. The war is already here. Blink and you'll miss it."

"Are you backing the Boston family too? Are you working with Orlando Green?"

Castor pushes back from the table and stands, methodically placing the gloves on his hands.

"Orlando Green has his utility. But his methods are barbaric and outdated."

"Father, I believe he is behind the murders of the humans at the storage facility. Surely you heard about those? He painted my name in blood on the walls. He would use me to start war overnight."

"As I said, barbaric," Castor says.

Cicero grunts, his temper flaring. "This is yer son, Castor. He'll be tarred and feathered if the humans find out vampires murdered those poor souls. Do ye not care about yer son's safety?"

Castor sighs emphatically. "You do not need to be concerned with Orlando Green. He is a vindictive brute, but he knows Elias is my son and therefore he cannot touch him. Or he will risk my anger."

Cicero sighs. "So that's it then? Elias doesn't need to worry about Boston? But what about a war? The humans could still find out about the murders."

"Leave the situation to me, Cicero." Castor sets his eyes on Eli's brooding face. "Elias, even though you have been a son long absent, you are still my son. It is my duty as Father to protect you."

Eli nods grimly. "Thank you, Father."

"Elias, I noticed your sober companion is not with you this evening," Castor says. "Is something wrong?"

"Nothing is wrong."

"Ah. That is good to hear. Because you would have me thinking young Eric is ill or something."

"Father, please be honest with me. Do you truly wish to start a war? Will you not help your oldest son stop a catastrophe? Where do your intentions lie? Do you not still consider me your blood? Your family?"

"Elias, you are my son. But you choose to sin against your father and against your family. A good parent corrects his child's misbehaviors. How else will you learn?"

He smiles smugly before turning and making his departure from the restaurant.

Eli stares hard at the table, stunned.

"Bloody hell!" Cicero exclaims. "How does he know about Eric?"

"I do not know," Eli says, shaking his head slowly. "He likes to mess with my head, he always has. I never have understood why."

"I do," Cicero says, taking a swig of Scotch. "It's because he's jealous."

"Jealous? Of what?"

"He knows ye're the better man. Ye always have been and always will be."

Eli raps his fingers on the table. "I really think it is him," he says. "I think Castor has worked his way through the system and he is prepared to push the big red button, so to speak."

"You think he's the one Frankie talked about? That he's in cahoots with Orlando Green, loosely, at least, but in cahoots all the same?"

"Yes, that is what I must conclude."

"What do you think will be his first move?"

"I wish I knew. But from the sound of it, perhaps he has already made it."

The next night when Eli brings Eric's dinner down into the cellar, he is pleased to find Eric cognizant and sane. But with the chemicals completely out of Eric's system, Eli is aware that he must now exercise extreme caution since he can smell Eric's blood.

Eli stops at the bottom of the cellar stairs and sets down the tray of food. He stands in the shadows, watching Eric rouse from a light nap.

"Hey," Eric says, voice drowsy. He sits up and leans against the wall. "Oh, man. My head hurts. But I think it's over."

Eli nods. "Yes. I believe you are clean."

Eric stands. "Good, because I'd like to sleep in my bed. A blanket on a dirt cellar floor just doesn't make for restful sleep."

"Yes, of course," Eli says.

Wary, he takes the key from its hook on the wall and approaches Eric. His blood scent grows stronger with proximity. "How do you feel?" He unlocks the thick handcuff.

"Not too bad. Mostly worn out," Eric says.

"I am sorry for this."

"Don't be. I was a maniac. You did me a favor."

"Come on. I'm sure you want out of this dank basement," Eli says.

"Yes. And I'd also like to know why you had a chain in the cellar."

Eli grins. "It is mandated by the board. All vampires in rehab must have a method to restrain themselves should the need arise."

Unable to keep himself from deeply inhaling the subtle scent of fresh blood circulating in the air, Eli fills with dread. He is dismayed as he feels his fangs slide out. He stuffs his fist in his mouth and lightly bites down hoping an infliction of pain will distract him from the tempting aroma. This is nothing like being around other humans. Eric's scent is an intoxicating mix of blood and pheromones unlike anyone else, save for Elizabeth when they were in the thralls of lovemaking.

Eric starts to go up the stairs but notices Eli's sudden, odd behavior. He trails him into the kitchen.

"What's wrong?"

Facing away from him, Eli shakes his head. "It's nothing," he lies. He stands at the table and gazes out the large rectangular window into the dark, still street.

Eric comes to his side and peers around in an attempt to see

113

his expression.

"Please step away," Eli says quickly.

"What is wrong?" Eric remains, trying to read his face.

Eric pulls on Eli's arm, a move that inadvertently sets him off. Eli turns and advances on him as hunger for live blood ignites. Eric grunts as he attempts to resist, a losing battle as he finds himself being pushed against the kitchen counter.

"Whoa, whoa! Calm down, Eli, calm down!" He sees Eli's fangs and watches as his dark eyes glaze over. "This is just a trigger. We can handle this!"

With hunger consuming his mind and body, Eli struggles to restrain himself. "Sorry. I am trying!" he says, gritting his teeth.

With Eric pinned against the counter, his prey is without an avenue of escape. Eli leans his head into the crook of Eric's neck, breathing in the scent of blood circulating just inches away.

"A little help here, sober companion! I feel a relapse coming on!" Eli says.

"Yeah, okay, just slow down and remember your rehab. Remember that you have a choice not to relapse. Are you with me?" Eric demands.

"You want transparency right?" Eli squeaks out.

"Yes, transparency is good. What are you feeling right now?" He leans as far away as he can from the vampire but realizes he is a mouse in a trap at the mercy of a starving cat.

"I really want to bite into your neck right now," Eli says.

"Okay, I understand." Eric hides his own panic. "But you can choose not to, okay? You are strong enough to overcome the urge!"

Eli pauses for a moment, then shakes his head. "I'm not feeling very strong right now!"

"All right. Let's try something, okay?"

"Okay … just please hurry," Eli whispers sharply.

"Close your eyes," Eric says.

"What? That's your plan? I'm losing it here, Eric!"

"Do you trust me?"

"Yes."

"Then close your eyes."

Eli growls and closes his eyes.

"Now think of something that makes you feel happy, and relaxed. Think of something that makes you feel whole, and complete. Relax into a fulfilling memory."

"Uh, okay, okay, I'm thinking, I'm thinking … is this really going to work?"

"Focus, Eli! You can do it."

Eric's blood smell and the warmth of his breath brushing past his face reminds Eli of one of the many bright, romantic afternoons spent with Elizabeth. He imagines her face, her enthralling smile, and the music of her voice. So many days were spent together, playing outside in nature teasing each other and reveling in each other's company. They are his favorite memories of her. The air was clean, the sun bright, her beauty radiant.

Eric can feel Eli relax against him, his near death grip on his arms weakening.

"Good. That's good," he says in a calm tone. "Keep doing that."

Eli's eyes remain closed as he allows himself to slip into memories of Elizabeth. The blood lust wanes, and the raging hunger loses its edge. His fangs retract as he continues to relax.

"Now, tell me what made it stop. What were you thinking of?"

"Elizabeth," Eli breathes.

Eli opens his eyes and pulls back, unaware that his mouth has been resting on Eric's jugular. He still feels the hunger, but it is sufficiently subdued. While leaning over his missed meal, he struggles not to lose himself in the same blue eyes he has loved for a thousand years.

"Eli?" Eric says. "Are you okay now?"

"I let you down. I am so sorry. I do not know how to make it stop."

"Make what stop, Eli? The craving? You just overcame it. You did it!"

"No," Eli says, forcing himself to back away. "Not the craving. Elizabeth."

Eric straightens and steps away from the counter, rubbing the ruts in his back left by the wood.

"This is the second time you mentioned that name. Do you want to talk about her?"

"I ... I do not know," Eli says with sadness in his voice.

"Sit down. I will warm up some synthetic, then you can tell me about this Elizabeth, all right?"

Eli proceeds to tell Eric the story of him and Elizabeth, and how the witch Moriah cursed them the night she found them sneaking off together. He tells him about the thousand years of Elizabeth's reincarnation, how she always dies in her twenty fifth year of life, and about the mark on her arm. But Eli leaves out the crucial piece of information that Eric is most likely Elizabeth's reincarnate. He cannot bring himself to tell him yet.

"But she doesn't know who you are each time she is reincarnated? You have to find her and get her to fall in love with you all over again?" Eric says.

"Yes."

"Hasn't she ever ... I don't know, run away screaming?"

Eli laughs. "Unfortunately, yes."

"How does she die?"

"Violently," Eli says. "Every time it is violently. Usually at the hands of a vampire."

"Wow. That is unbelievable," Eric says. "It is sad to think she doesn't remember you though."

"Well ... that's not precisely true. She does remember me, but only when she is in the process of dying."

"What do you mean?"

"Each time she sustains the mortal wound, she looks at me and says, *I remember!* Every life time, every reincarnation, all the way back to the night of the curse. She remembers it all. She remembers how I have loved her. And then, she dies."

"My god. That's terrible," Eric says.

They sit quietly for a long moment, Eric soaking in the information while Eli tries to understand his feelings for the reincarnation of Elizabeth that sits in front of him.

"So this witch … Moriah? You're still trying to find her, to break the curse?"

"I have failed miserably in the endeavor."

"Even if you were to find her, do you think she would do the right thing and break it?"

"Honestly, I do not."

"Then what are your other options?"

"I have none."

Eric's hand mindlessly floats to his own shoulder, the one with the mark. "Eli. You were curious about the birthmark on my shoulder. Do you believe there is some connection between me and Elizabeth? Did she ever have children? Maybe I am a descendant or something?"

Eli smiles. "There were a few life cycles that I was not able to find her. Anything is possible, I suppose."

"Maybe that is why I felt like I knew you when we first met. Some sort of cosmic familial connection," Eric states, pondering what he's learned.

"Perhaps," Eli says.

"So what do we do now?"

"About what?"

"About your sobriety, and about me violating my court order to take the chemicals?"

Eli stands and walks to the window, peering again into the darkness. "We tell no one of your status, and we deal with any issues affecting my sobriety as they come. Simple."

"You will be persecuted if they find out you're covering for me," Eric warns.

"We are in this together, Eric. I will not have it any other way."

Chapter Ten

"He made his move!" Cicero shouts as he pushes his way through the front door the next morning. "Did you read today's headlines?" He shoves the morning newspaper at Eli.

"No, I've been in the study all night," he says. He reads the headlines of the *New York Times out loud. "Explosions at chemical plants annihilate synthetic blood supply. Dear God!"

"This has got to be Castor's doing!" Cicero exclaims.

"Cicero! If this is true, the sobriety program just crashed and burned."

"Yep. I know. It's just as we feared."

"Only I cannot believe it's happened so fast. How can this be?"

Cicero picks up Eric's blood scent before he enters the kitchen.

"Come in, lad, join the meltdown," Cicero says.

Eric approaches slowly to gauge the probability that his presence will trigger Eli's raging hunger. Luckily, the shock of the morning news seems to have him sufficiently distracted.

"What's going on?"

"Oh, just the beginning of the end," Cicero groans, slumping into a chair at the table.

Eric pulls out a chair and sits as Eli hands him the newspaper.

"Holy shit! Is this real?" Eric says, eyes wide.

"It is real, Eric," Eli says.

Eric reads the headlines several times and looks at Eli. "What does this mean, though? I mean, surely they have reserves of synthetic in case of emergency, right?"

"I do not know. Perhaps David Carey knows," Eli says. He removes his cell from his pocket and calls the parole officer, flipping on the speakerphone as David answers.

"Elias?" David answers the phone.

"Yes, David. This is Elias. Do you know why I am calling?"

"Yes, you and at least a hundred other clients so far this morning," David says, his voice thin from having been talking to distraught clients all morning.

"David, please tell me there are reserves of synthetic for a disaster such as this?"

"Elias, I wish I could. There are none."

"Excuse me?" Eric chimes in. "How is there no contingency plan? The sobriety program cannot exist without synthetic!"

"It's worse than you think," David says. "The chemical plants that manufacture the synthetic also produce the chemical injections that mask the blood scent for sober companions and humans serving in other capacities close to vampires. The entire system is offline."

"David, what can be done? Tell me how I can help and I will do anything," Eli says.

A long pause on David's end of the call tells them everything they need to know.

"David?"

"Pray," David says finally, his voice thick with desperation. "Elias, pray."

The line clicks as David hangs up.

"Christ in heaven," Cicero murmurs.

Eli's phone buzzes with a news text alert. He opens the

internet browser to a live broadcast of the President's speech.

"The President is speaking on this," Eli says. He holds the phone out for Eric and Cicero to see and increases the volume all the way.

The President's somber mood is evident by her body posture and tout facial expression. Photographers in the crowd snap flashes as she, the first African-American female elected to the presidency, moves the microphone at the podium closer to her mouth. The American flag hangs flat in the background. The President gently clears her throat and the press falls quiet.

"My fellow Americans," she begins. "Many of you are already aware of the terrorist attack on multiple chemical plants in this country. Specifically, these plants are the manufacturers of synthetic blood and chemicals that have made this country's vampire sobriety program possible. I regret to inform you that these attacks have rendered the supply of these products completely vanquished."

Eli, Eric, and Cicero exchange looks, silently share their apprehension of what this means for their world as they know it.

"I first want to assure you that we will bring these terrorists to justice," the President continues.

Cicero snorts. "Good luck with that."

"And secondly, our top federal government officials are actively collaborating with all states to reach a contingency plan for this crisis. I can assure you. We will reach an effective resolution, but due to the sheer size of the sobriety program, we ask for your patience as we navigate this issue together, as a country."

"That's politician speak for *we got nothin'*," Cicero says.

"In the meantime, I have been advised to urge all vampires currently dependent on the synthetic product to kindly avoid humans to the best of your ability, and to continue to report to your parole officers as scheduled. I have also been advised to urge all sober companions to cease and desist your service to vampires in the program, for your own safety."

"Cease and desist," Eric repeats in a whisper.

"Looks like we got you detoxed just in time," Eli says quietly.

"Humans and vampires, your government is working hard on this issue, and your continued patience and cooperation is called for. We will provide you with updates as we have them. Thank you, and God bless the United States of America."

The press erupts in questions for the President, but she quickly leaves the podium without answering them. The video feed ends.

Eli closes the internet browser on his phone and lays it on the table. The three stare at it, stewing in their shock.

"Well, today went to hell in a hand basket," Cicero says finally.

Eli shakes his head. "I cannot believe he did it," he says. The comment piques Eric's curiosity.

"Who?"

Surprised by his own thoughtlessness, Eli looks up from the table and wishes he had guarded his words.

"Now ye've done it," Cicero says through pursed lips. Anticipating the impending altercation, he twists in his chair to face the window.

Eric narrows his eyes and glares at Eli. "You know who did this?"

Eli stares at Cicero, desperate for help, but receives none.

"Eli?" Eric says, his voice filling with anger.

"I believe so, yes," Eli answers.

Eric shoves himself away from the table and stands up to pace the floor.

"How long have you known this was going to happen?"

Eli holds up his hands. "Eric, it has only been a few days since I had a clue of the possibility -"

Eric pivots abruptly and storms out of the kitchen.

"Eric!" Eli gets up and follows him into the foyer. "I did not know this would happen so soon!"

"So soon?"

"Cicero and I met with him last night, and it was only then we started honing in on his intentions!"

Eric holds out his arms waiting for a better explanation. "Who? Who are you talking about?"

"My ... uh, my father," Eli says, grimacing at how incriminating his words are.

"Your *father*?" Eric snorts.

His face rapidly flushes a bright shade of red as his anger builds. Eli hears the heavy pounding of his heart.

"Eric, maybe you should calm down," Eli says.

With increased circulation comes the fresh stirring of Eric's blood scent and pheromones in the air. The smell begins to pique Eli's appetite.

Cicero smells it too, but given that he still live blood feeds, he maintains better control over his hunger. His concern is maintaining control over Eli.

"Elias, pal," Cicero says, jumping up from the kitchen chair and following Eli into the foyer. "Maybe we should go out for a walk. What do you say? Get some fresh air?"

"So you're telling me your father destroyed the chemical supply, and now we're going to war because of it?"

"Eric, please calm down," Eli says, feeling himself break into the vampire equivalent of a cold sweat. "Please, all I can think about right now is your blood."

"Are you involved in this, Eli?" Eric demands, rushing the vampire and stopping just inches away from him. "Because if you are in any way involved with this, I will call David right now and have you taken away."

Cicero grabs Eli's arm and tries to pull him back. "Elias!" He warns.

Eli breathes deeply, trying to calm his inner beast demanding to be released.

"Eric, look I am sorry. I am not involved in this, I swear," he says. The tunnel vision that accompanies severe hunger attacks starts to form. "You are triggering my hunger. Will you please calm yourself!"

"Is this what you do? Do violence and destruction follow you everywhere you go? First it's the Boston thing, now the chemical supply? Is everyone in the world after Elias Alexander? Do you attract evil and destruction? Because I don't want any part of this kind of life. Court ordered or not, I refuse to enable you in whatever it is you do!"

"What is wrong with you?" Eli growls. "You are accusing me of being responsible for the murders and the terror attacks?"

"You're obviously a key player in this, Eli! If you're so innocent, why don't you *do* something? It's evident you have the clout and the power to jump in and try to save what semblance of peace there still is! Do something, for God's sake!"

Overwrought by the escalating tension between vampire and sober companion, Cicero pulls harder at Eli's arm. "Elias, ye need to back off," Cicero pleads. "Please, before -"

"Before what, Cicero?" Eric yells. "Before he does something? I would be glad to see him *do* something instead of just sitting back and watching the world rage around him."

Eli jerks his arm out of Cicero's grasp and steps towards the seething human.

"What do you know about me, Eric?" He grabs Eric by the shirt collar. "You do not know me!"

"It doesn't take a genius to make a few key observations," Eric says tersely. "Where is your resolve? Where is your passion? Are you loyal to a father that would see us into war? Are you really that docile now? Just let everything be as it may? What the hell have you ever really fought for, anyway? All you do is wait around for life to happen the way you want it to! Everyone and everything else be damned!"

Eric shoves at the vampire but is unable to detach from him.

"What have I fought for? How can you even ask me that? I told you what has kept me going the past thousand years!"

"Yeah, a girl that you'll never be able to have," Eric shouts. "You're a really slow learner, Eli, if you think she's going to change after a millennium of making the same choice to die instead of stay with you!"

Enraged, Eli punches Eric in the face with a force that sends him flying backwards onto the hardwood floor. He hears the bones in Eric's cheek and eye socket crack and smells the blood before it seeps out of the deep gash in Eric's eyebrow.

"Elias!" Cicero screams. He rushes to grab Eli just as he pins Eric to the floor, and wrenches him up to prevent him from making a meal out of the bleeding boy.

Resisting Cicero's iron grasp, Eli presses down towards Eric, his fangs out as his hunger is fully ignited.

Engulfed in his own fit of rage, Eric struggles against the rabid vampire and manages to sock him hard in the face.

"Get off me!" he yells.

"You think I don't fight for anything? You think all I do is wait around? Do you want to know what I've been waiting for, Eric?"

Eric socks him again, this time fracturing the bones in his hand. He screams at the pain. "God damn it! Get off me!"

"Elias get ahold of yerself!" Cicero pleads.

"You want transparency, Eric Wayne? I'll give you transparency. It's you!"

Enraged and hurting, Eric wrestles with all his might to get away but fails miserably.

"What the hell are you talking about?"

"I've been waiting for you!" Eli rips the collar of Eric's long sleeve shirt to expose the birthmark on his shoulder. "This is the mark of the witch Moriah! It is no birthmark. It is a curse! You are Elizabeth! You look just like her. You bear the mark, and everything you do reminds me of her! You're twenty five years old and your time is running out. You *will* die soon!"

Eric's struggling wanes, but he is now angry and confused. "I

… I don't believe you," he says.

"Do you want something to believe?" He growls. "All I can think about right now is draining every last ounce of your blood!" Eli grimaces as raging hunger and moral dilemma battle for control of him. "I want to drink you dry and make you mine for the rest of eternity. Is that enough transparency for you, Eric Wayne?"

"Don't ye dare bite into him, Elias," Cicero warns. "If ye do it'll go against everything ye've worked for yer entire life!"

"Is this what you did to Elizabeth?" Eric says, grimacing. "Did you feed off her and try to force her into letting you turn her?"

"I never touched her!"

"It's true, lad," Cicero says, grunting as his grip on Eli begins to slip. "He never fed off her. He wouldn't do that."

"And you, Cicero? Are you backing him up on this? That somehow I'm the same person he's been waiting for all this time?"

"We are as surprised as ye, lad," Cicero says with a grunt.

With every cell in his body wanting to plunge his fangs into what would surely be the most delicious delicacy there ever was, Eli's conscience gets the better of him.

"Eric, get up," he says, his voice strained.

"What? I can't, you're holding me down!"

"Get out from under me and get up. Then get the hell out of this house before I lose my one last ounce of restraint!"

"Do as he says, lad!" Cicero says.

Cicero tightens his grip on Eli and holds him back as Eric pulls himself out from underneath him and staggers onto his feet. Blood pours freely from the gash in Eric's face and a few drops hit the floor.

Eli's restraint continues towards failure. "Cicero, I cannot stop myself! I want to know once and for all and his blood remnants will tell me!" He says, bargaining for Eric's blood out of both hunger and desperation to know if he truly is Elizabeth's reincarnation.

Eli jerks out of Cicero's grasp and rushes Eric before he even has time to turn and run. He shoves him against the wall of the staircase, but Cicero grabs him before he can feed.

Eric's anger has transformed into fear as he watches the benevolent, peaceful vampire he has come to idolize turn into a voracious creature before his eyes.

"I will make you stay this time," Eli says, his hunger and frustration blinding his judgment. "I will *make you stay!*"

"I see your true colors, Eli," Eric says through gritted teeth. "You're nothing but a monster!"

"Let him go, Elias, I'm warnin' ye," Cicero shouts. "Now!"

Through Eli's animalistic urges, he sees the frightened face of the beautiful soul he has nothing but love for and he feels his heart break.

"Go now," he manages in a whisper. He turns his head to Cicero. "Cicero, the cellar," he says. "Hurry."

Before Eric can get in another breath, Eli and Cicero speed into the cellar so that Eric will be out of imminent danger. Eric watches the door slam behind them and pulls himself away from the wall. He touches his wound with the back of his hand and stares in horror at the smudge of blood on it. Painfully aware that Eli could bust out of the cellar and attack him in a blood thirsty frenzy, Eric runs upstairs to his room. He frantically packs his bag, not bothering to close the drawers of the dresser and nightstand after pulling out the clothes from it. With no time to properly sort and fold his belongings, he instead shoves everything in and has to lean on the bag to help it zip closed.

He runs down the stairs, glancing nervously back at the cellar door and around the foyer for any sign of Eli before jumping the last two steps and sprinting towards the front door. In his haste he doesn't notice the figures standing outside the door and nearly trips over his own feet as he pulls it open and stops abruptly.

Captain Meyers and two police officers stand stone-faced at the door. The Captain notices Eric's bleeding wound and glares.

"Eric Wayne, we're here to take you into custody," Captain Meyers says.

"What? Why?"

"Due to the terror attacks on the chemical plants, the sober companion program is no longer intact. You are to finish out your court ordered sentence for the murder of a Vampire-American in state prison."

An officer takes Eric's bag from him while the other comes around behind him to apply handcuffs.

"Wait, Captain please. The attacks just happened! Don't I have time to take this to an appeals court?"

"Not when martial law is coming into force," Captain Meyers says.

"Martial law?" Eric says in disbelief.

Overhearing the conversation, Eli and Cicero emerge from the cellar. The new development distracts Eli from his hunger frenzy. His fangs retract and his mind clears.

"Captain?" Eli calls as he and Cicero approach the door.

The two officers begin to lead Eric down the stairs to their squad car.

"I am obligated to inform you that by order of the Governor of the State of New York, martial law is now in effect. All vampires must remain indoors indefinitely. Leaving your residence will result in imprisonment. Any willful acts of violence against humans will result in the loss of your life." The Captain regards Eli with an expression that strangely seems concerned. "Tough break, Alexander," he says as he turns and heads to the squad car.

"Where are you taking the boy?" Cicero asks.

"Straight to prison, gentlemen. Straight to prison," the Captain answers.

Guilt engulfs Eli as Eric glances at him while the police put him in the back seat of the police car. He looks afraid.

Cicero glances down the street at the tank slowly rounding the corner, flanked by a half dozen armed National Guard members. Humans come out of their homes and huddle together in the street. The typically peaceful, upscale Greenwich Village neighborhood is already starting to look like the beginnings of a civil war.

"Come inside, Elias," Cicero says, pulling Eli back inside and closing the door.

Eli drags his fingers through his hair and groans in frustration.

"Bloody hell, Elias. How can this be happening so fast?" Cicero says.

"There's only one explanation for this. It was all planned. Every last detail. Every last minute," Eli says, knocking the coat rack next to the door onto the floor. "I cannot believe I have been so blind!"

"This wasn't yer fault, lad! Ye had nothin' to do with it!"

"That might be true, but Eric is right. I should have been paying attention. I should be using my pull in the vampire community to ensure something like this never happens. I am at fault for this, just like he said."

Cicero grumbles and groans. He trails Eli into the kitchen where they watch the tank and National Guardsmen slowly clear the street outside. A police car follows behind running its lights and while an officer's voice reverberates over the loud speaker.

"Attention residents. Martial law is now in effect. Humans have a mandatory curfew. Please return to your homes by sundown. Vampires are ordered to remain indoors. A violation of this martial law will result in persecution at the full extent of the law."

"They are terrified," Eli mumbles.

"What's that?"

"The humans. They are afraid the vampires on the sobriety program will go mad with hunger and start killing."

"They wouldn't be far off, Elias. That's likely to happen. I think we both know that."

"Yes," Eli says. He replays the confrontation with Eric in his mind and chastises himself for letting his hunger get the best of him. He doesn't realize Cicero is staring at him.

"Can't ye still smell that?"

"Hmm?" Eli says, stirring from the volatile thoughts.

Cicero turns and points to the floor in the foyer. "The blood," he says quietly. "On the floor. If ye want to know for certain, now's yer chance."

Eli's gaze lands on the bright red drops of Eric's blood. He shakes his head as the tunnel vision starts to cloud his eyes. In a trance he slowly walks to the blood, stopping a few feet away from it and inhaling the aroma deeply.

Cicero watches his friend stand and stare for an oddly long time. "Well?"

With hunger cravings dissipated, Eli's morality will not allow him to take in Eric's blood without his permission. He shakes his head and retreats back into the kitchen.

"I cannot, Cicero. It would not be right."

Cicero grins and gazes fondly at him.

"What?" Eli says.

"This is who ye are, Elias. Yer true colors. Yer a good man."

Eli shrugs. "I was not good to Eric just moments ago. He called me a monster. Perhaps that is all I really am."

"It was the hunger, lad. It had a hold of ye, that's what it does." Cicero curses beneath his breath. "It seems like this whole system was set up just so it could be knocked over. The treachery runs deep."

"If Castor is the true mastermind behind this, then yes, it could not run deeper."

"Ach, what I wouldn't do for one of Frankie's concoctions right now," Cicero says, slumping down into a kitchen chair. "Served by that fine little lady, Dorothy. Wasn't she a cute one, Eli? Yeah, I could see us livin' happily ever after."

"Yes," Eli says with a chuckle.

While Cicero continues to ramble on about Dorothy, an idea hits Eli like a spark of lightning.

"Yes!" Eli shouts.

Cicero, annoyed by the interruption glares at him. "Yeah —

did ye hear anything I was sayin'? Are ye goin' daft now?"

"Frank! He's the answer!" Eli pulls out a chair and sits at the table next to him.

"The answer to what?"

"To the supply problem, to the synthetic!"

"How do you figure? Vampires aren't legally allowed to produce or sell anything."

"At this point, that doesn't matter. What matters is Frank knows how to replicate the synthetic formula. He can produce it for immediate release to area vampires! There is a chance we can stop this massive wave of relapsing vampires, at least in New York City."

"Okay, let's say he can produce it, how are we going to convince the human authorities to let him sell it?"

"I am not sure yet, but we will figure it out, Cicero."

"What if this doesn't work?"

"What other options are there? This thing is spiraling out of control, and fast. Anything we can do to stop the bleeding will be worth the risk."

Eli runs to the study and retrieves his cell phone. He returns to the kitchen and Cicero leans in as he makes a call to Frank.

"Wait! What about Eric? They're haulin' him off to prison now!"

Eli grimaces. "One thing at a time. We need to address the synthetic issue first, then we'll deal with him."

"How?"

"I don't know yet, Cicero. But if we don't stop this massive relapse wave, there may be no saving him anyway."

Chapter Eleven

Imprisoned for a week, Eric sits by himself at a table in the communal television room. His attention drifts from the live news streaming on the television to the appalling hue of his bright orange prison jumpsuit. He wrestles with guilt from having accused Eli of being nothing more than a monster. He realizes now that it was too much pressure for Eli to handle living with a full blood-scent human while struggling to maintain his sobriety. The program was designed to be effective when vampires are paired with sober companions they couldn't smell so as not to tempt them. Eric can't help but blame himself for becoming addicted to the chemical injections, even if it wasn't his fault. Purging his addiction to the chemicals is the reason Eli flipped out. It's the reason they are now separated on bad terms, and Eric has no idea what is happening to Eli under the new martial law.

And what if Eli was right about Eric's life being in danger of ending soon? If he really is the reincarnation of a soul cursed by a witch, and he is supposed to die in his twenty fifth year of life, then how long does he have to live?

"Hey, turn it up!"

The inmate's shout interrupts Eric's spiraling thoughts and he looks up at the television as an inmate turns up the volume. A press conference on CNN shows a breaking news interview with a vampire named Castor.

A female news anchor interviews him. "So, Mr. Castor, can you give our viewers an idea of how the vampire community plans to handle this very delicate and ever-changing situation?"

"It is simple, Patricia. Our community is united. We are

resolute upon finding an acceptable solution to the sudden shortage of synthetic supply. As the oldest member of my community, I propose to our government that we immediately begin rewriting vampire policy in this country in an effort to defray any negative repercussions of this horrific terror attack within the vampire community."

"Mr. Castor, am I correct to conclude that you wish to initiate, for lack of a better word, a political reset button for vampire policy?"

"What better time is there than in a crisis to restructure policy to the benefit of all members of society?"

"Some may say this is jumping the gun a bit, Mr. Castor," the female anchor says.

"Yes, Patricia, but if the vampire and human communities continue to work together on improving policy, what do we have to lose? Look, we face a nationwide relapse by millions of vampires. Human and vampire lives alike are at risk here. Let us work together to be sure both races have equal access to the resources they need. Let us work together on this problem. With my leadership on this issue, the public can rest assured that the vampire community is doing everything within its power to ensure the safety of human lives."

"Mr. Castor, how exactly do you propose to fashion and carry out new vampire policy?"

"Simple, Patricia. I urge the American public to vote me into a position where I can be most effective. I plan to enter the next Senatorial race."

"You're running for Senator? Even though current American policy prohibits vampires from voting, let alone from running for political office! Mr. Castor, what you are suggesting has never been done before!"

"Yes, Patricia. But crisis calls for change. Because of the terror attacks and the looming vampire relapse, it is time to expand our minds and begin thinking in a new direction."

"One moment … I'm sorry, we have another breaking news story coming out of New York City," she says. She listens to the producer's new instructions coming through the microphone in her ear. "CNN's Ashley Taylor has the breaking news for us … Ashley, can you hear me?"

The screen flips to a beautiful young Filipino-American reporter.

"Yes, Patricia I hear you."

"Ashley, tell us what's going on in Manhattan?"

"Patricia, I'm standing in front of a very old, members-only club called the Maverick here in Manhattan. Joining me is Mr. Elias Alexander, who happens to be one of the oldest vampires alive. Now, I know what you're thinking, how can a vampire be out on the streets? Well, Mr. Alexander has obtained permission from the Governor's office to postpone his own curfew under the close observation of Captain Meyers of the NYPD."

Eric tensely watches the scene unfold in disbelief. The screen is still split between the vampire Castor and the scene in Manhattan with Eli. Castor is visibly angered.

"Mr. Alexander, can you explain exactly what is going on behind me?" She holds the microphone out for him.

"Yes, Ashley," Eli says.

Eric notices that Eli appears confident and energetic, a stark difference to the hungry, conflicted Eli that wanted to drink his blood last week.

"It's a great thing, really. My good friend has been able to replicate the chemical compounds in synthetic blood and produce a new version of the drink. The only difference is in the taste. As any vampire knows that has gone through the rehab program and drinks synthetic blood, the taste of the original recipe was terrible!"

Ashley giggles at Eli's animated presentation of facts.

"But what my friend has done is amazing, he's found a way to make the drink taste good while retaining the properties that provide nourishment to vampires and keep us satiated."

"This is amazing, Mr. Alexander," Ashley says. "How much and how long, in terms of production, do you anticipate being able to get this supply circulating in the country?"

"We're still working out all the details, but we believe Manhattan will be adequately resupplied within a week, and right now we're sharing the chemical compounds with contacts in every state willing to give the product a chance to work."

"So, what would you say to vampires right now, who might be hungry and relapsing?"

Eli looks into the camera and holds a regal posture. "I say this to vampires everywhere. You can be hopeful that sustenance is on its way and very soon. In the meantime, I'm asking you to use great restraint. Remember the techniques you used in rehab to stay relaxed when you are overcome by a triggering event. You can do this. We will get through this together. And from now on, you will have me as a resource every step of the way."

"Mr. Alexander, do you think your status in the vampire community will help this project to be successful?"

"Ashley, a friend of mine recently opened my eyes to the fact that my station in this life has an impact, and it's either going to be valuable or pointless, depending on how I choose to use it. So I choose to make it count. I am here to support all vampires and to let humans know that we truly want peace, just as you do, and I will do anything I can to preserve the peace between us."

"This is Ashley Taylor in Manhattan. Patricia, back to you."

Animated conversation among inmates erupts in the communal room and drowns out the rest of the interview with Castor on the television.

Eric is filled with pride. He taps a finger on the table and grins, shaking his head as he comes to terms with the fact that Eli is finally standing up for something.

"You're doing it," he says quietly. "Way to go, you jerk!" He smiles to himself.

The bell rings and the guards herd the inmates back into their jail cells. To his utter relief, so far Eric has a cell to himself. As allowed in the evening, Eric changes out of the orange jumpsuit and into a white T-shirt and grey sleeping pants, the prison's version of pajamas. After a few hours of pacing, doing pushups and sit ups, and staring at the ugly bare cement brick walls, he lays down on the poor excuse for a bed and allows his thoughts to flow freely. Soon, a guard passes calling for lights out, and the lights dim on all floors of the prison. Dim emergency lighting glows at exits but for the most part, there is only darkness.

For the first time since the terror attacks on the chemical plants, Eric feels hopeful about the future. With Eli stepping up for the vampire community, he thinks there is a chance a second war can be avoided. It's just too bad he won't be able to help, given that he'll be in prison for the next two years.

Two years. Reality sinks in. Eric smacks himself in the forehead and rolls over on the bunk bed to face the wall. He much preferred being a sober companion during the first three years of his sentence, but serving two years in prison seems extremely daunting.

"Holy shit," he grumbles. "Two years."

He closes his eyes, hoping to fall asleep fast so that he can stop thinking about his lengthy stay in prison. But for hours deep into the night he manages only to toss and turn as he wrestles with feelings of helplessness and frustration. Sometime around two in the morning, sleep finally begins to win and he dozes. A nightmare ensues and he awakens to the sight of a dark form standing at the barred door of his cell.

After blinking rapidly and rubbing his eyes, the dark figure remains, peering in at him. He sits up fast and strains to get a look at the observer.

"Who are you?" he whispers. A pocket of cold air sends a chill through his body.

"Eric," the figure whispers.

Eric's heart skips a beat. He doesn't recognize the voice, but it is unusually deep.

"What do you want?"

"I know what you did," he says. "*Vampire killer.*"

Eric jumps out of the bed and backs up to the stone wall.

"What the hell do you want?"

To his horror, he hears the sound of a key slide into the lock on the cell door. It seems as though the figure intentionally jiggles the key to elicit fear from him. The dark figure chuckles.

"I want you dead, vampire killer," he says.

Eric hears the door slide open and shouts. "Guard!"

The form rushes in and pins him against the wall while clamping a cold hand over his mouth before he can scream again. Eric can tell his attacker is a vampire from the speed with which he moves, his brute strength, and cold skin.

"If it were up to me, I would kill you right now," the vampire says. "But I'm under orders to bring you in first."

Eric's screams catch in his covered mouth and the vampire drives a knee into his stomach to silence him. The hard blow knocks the wind out of him, and he can feel the impact from the vampire's knee all the way through to his spine.

"Time to go," the vampire hisses.

The vampire snaps Eric's head back against the wall, the blow knocking him out.

When he comes to, he is no longer in the state prison, but he is still a prisoner.

He sits up from a thin mat on a hard cement floor and grabs the back of his head, groaning as a sharp pain shoots through it. His vision blackens and he closes his eyes to stave off the threat of nausea. After a moment the pain lessens and he opens his eyes to survey the strange new surroundings.

The room is small and square with a cement floor and walls. A single florescent light hangs from the ceiling. There are no windows and there is no natural light save for that coming from the bottom of the knobless door.

"What the hell?"

He remembers being attacked in his prison cell, but he doesn't know by whom, and he definitely doesn't know where he is now. He looks at the sticky blood on his palm and grimaces.

"Damn it," he says, touching the sore spot on his head and removing more blood from it.

He hears the door unlock from the outside and stands up fast, regretting his haste as his vision clouds over again. He leans over and hangs his head in an attempt to clear the sudden blood rush.

"How do you like your new accommodations?"

The voice is familiar.

Eric blinks his vision clear and leans against the wall. "You're Jeremiah?"

Jeremiah nods. "I'm surprised you remember me after I bashed in your brains last night," he says with a smirk.

Eric feels the bloody spot on his head again but stops abruptly, concerned that Jeremiah might be lured into a blood frenzy.

Jeremiah cocks his head to the side. "I'm not allowed to feed on you. They're saving you for someone special."

"Where the hell am I? What's going on?" Eric demands.

"Shhh," Jeremiah says with a sneer. "It will all make sense soon, boy."

"How did you know I killed a vampire?"

Jeremiah walks towards him and stops just feet away. Eric tries to lean away from him but the brick wall at his back prevents him from making more distance between them.

"He was a friend, you see," Jeremiah says, leering in Eric's face. "And *you* killed him."

"He attacked my girlfriend. He was relapsing! I had no choice. I had to defend her."

Jeremiah pokes his finger into Eric's stomach. "How's that rib?" He says.

Having been focused on the pain in his head, Eric hadn't noticed that his stomach and right ribs are also sore. He winces as Jeremiah pokes him.

Jeremiah grins. "How about if I even things out for you?"

"What?"

With a speed faster than Eric's eyes can follow, Jeremiah lands two hard strikes to both sides of his ribs, cracking them. The pain is overwhelming and he falls to his knees on the hard floor.

Jeremiah laughs and watches Eric gasp and cough as he tries to overcome the pain of having all of his ribs cracked at once.

"They said I couldn't feed on you. But they told me to keep you tenderized," he taunts.

Eric holds his ribs and struggles to breathe normally, fearing his lungs could be bruised from the brutal hits. "Who is behind this? What do they want?"

Jeremiah backs away from him and shrugs. "You're just a piece of bait, little boy," he says. "How does that feel?"

"Bait? For what?"

Jeremiah pounds on the door. It opens. "I wish I could tell you not to be scared. But you really should be. You're going to die, vampire killer. Horribly."

Relieved that Jeremiah leaves, but dealing with more pain and confusion, Eric sits against the wall and curses in frustration. This prison might be worse than the first one. He is obviously being held captive by hostile vampires, and things probably couldn't get much worse.

The birthmark on his arm suddenly ignites with a supernatural heat. He jumps and grabs at it, pulling up the sleeve of his T-shirt so he can see it. Something is making it hot, but he doesn't know what. The heat is equivalent to that of a second degree sunburn, uncomfortable but manageable.

"What the hell is going on?" He asks with no one to hear him.

Chapter Twelve

Late at night after a long day of helping Frank with the manufacturing and distributing of Salvation, Eli and Cicero slump down in chairs at the kitchen table.

"I really blew it with Eric," Eli says.

"Give him time," Cicero advises.

"It has been weeks. The prison still says he will not accept any communication from me."

"He's probably tryin' to deal with losing his freedom. It's nae an enjoyable thing, prison. Believe me, I speak from experience."

Eli glares at him. "You were locked up for three days."

"The three most miserable days of my life!"

Eli chuckles and sighs. "It's just that we left on bad terms. I don't want that."

"Maybe he's seen what ye're doin' on the television. Maybe he knows ye took his advice."

"Yes, perhaps. But this situation with the synthetic has taken up so much of my time, I haven't been able to work on a solution for him."

"Ye mean to save him before he dies," Cicero says grimly.

"Yes. I admit, I still feel conflicted about it. If I let him pass, there is the chance Elizabeth will come back as herself next."

"But since things are different this time, there's also the chance she won't."

"I know, Cicero. And Eric is … very special. I would be content to have him around for a long period of time."

"Just content? Ye'd better make up yer mind, Elias. Either ye turn him, or ye'll lose him for good. There's nae guarantee either of them will come back. What if Moriah's plan was to string ye along and end it all with Eric? Then after he's dead, there's nothin'? No more reincarnations, no more soul mate for ye. What if that's her plan?"

"We simply cannot know her plan," Eli says.

"Aye, but ye can do somethin' with what ye have now. Ye've the chance to keep him around."

"I know."

"Bah, whatever," Cicero says standing up. "I've enough of this. I'm gonna watch some television. You interested?"

Eli's phone buzzes with a text and he frowns as he reads it.

"Frank's shorthanded again," he says. "Says he could use my help."

"Well, let's go then."

"No, it's all right, Cicero. You have been working non-stop. Stay here and relax. I will go."

"I've nae worked any harder than ye!"

"I know, but this is kind of my project. Besides, you've earned a good break." He smiles warmly at his friend and grabs his coat from the rack by the front door. "Don't wait up!"

"Go forth and feed the vampires!" Cicero yells.

The police unit parked outside waves Eli on as he waves at them. His role as the leader in the vampire relapse prevention efforts has won him the freedom to walk in public, while other vampires are still ordered to stay indoors until the Salvation supply is more readily available.

As Eli arrives at the Maverick, he is surprised to find things very quiet. He makes his way to the large production room in the back of the building and sees Frank oddly standing still in the midst of boxed up product, waiting for him.

"Frank? Is everything okay? Why aren't the machines running? Where is the rest of the staff?"

"They were told to take a break," Frank says, his voice tight.

Eli notices the nervous expression on Frank's face. "What is wrong?"

"Hello, Eli."

Eli recognizes the voice coming from behind him. He scowls.

"Jeremiah," he says coldly. He turns to see Jeremiah along with Castor and six other vampires closing in on him. "Father? What is going on?"

"Surely you do not need to ask that, Elias," Castor responds.

Two vampires grab Eli's arms, restraining him.

"You are angry that I solved the food supply issue before you could rise to power," Eli says. "And subsequently avoided war."

"I would have lead the country away from war as well. I admit, your little stunt has forced me to make some minor modifications to my plans," he says, sneering at the boxes of Salvation. "However, I can manage it just fine. Bring him," he orders the vampires.

Eli attempts escape but his efforts are in vain. The vampires restraining him are at full strength and he has no chance to evade them.

"Burn it down," Castor says.

"No!" Frank cries out. "Not my facility, please! Castor, you promised!"

"I promised not to kill you, Frank Green. That is the extent of my word."

"Castor, do not do this! Frank is the proprietor of Salvation, we need him and this facility to feed Manhattan!" Eli exclaims.

"Manhattan is no longer your concern, Elias," Castor says.

"Bring him!"

"Eli, I am sorry," Frank laments.

"Frank, it will be all right. Find Cicero!"

"Cicero just received a message from a friend back home in Scotland in dire need of his help. He'll be adequately distracted, Elias. You will not be seeing him again," Castor says.

Eli's hands are bound with chains and he is blinded by a thick black hood placed over his head. He is thrown into a van and driven across the bridge to Castor's Brooklyn warehouse. The vampires drag him a great distance until finally removing the black hood but leaving the chains on his hands.

Eli glances around the small square room with cement floor and walls. There are no windows and the only break in the cement dreariness is the door that has no knob.

Castor enters the room behind four of the guard vampires.

"It has been an age since you experienced the Dry Death, Elias. Has it not?"

"What are you planning?" Eli growls.

Castor straightens the black leather gloves on his hands. "I am sure you remember how painful it is. When your veins run dry, how every breath you take feels gritty, like inhaling sandpaper."

"Damn it, Castor, do not do this! The vampire community needs my help. Our help! Will you not work with me, instead of against me? Why must you see everything concerning humans as a battle?"

"Because it *is* a battle!" Castor hisses. "We *are* at war with humans. We always have been! We cannot coexist. It is not in either of our natures! Both species want to be on top, yet there can be only one dominant race. The humans have outstayed their welcome in my world. I mean to submit them all. They will be pets and they will be food, nothing more."

Eli shakes his head. "It is sad, Father, that you cannot see beyond your own greed."

"Enjoy the Dry Death, Elias."

"Father!" Eli shouts.

Castor and the vampires leave, locking Eli in the room. The pain and discomfort of the Dry Death begin to take their toll after merely a week.

Four weeks after his abduction, Eli remains in solitary confinement, his hands bound, his mind betraying him as hallucinations from hunger and depravity set in.

Eli's mind fades in and out of cognizance. His thoughts drift to those that matter most to him. He wonders if Frank is devastated by the burning down of the Maverick. He worries about Cicero and if Castor set a trap for him as well. Memories of Elizabeth weave their way into his mind but thoughts of Eric are the most poignant in the midst of his delirium.

As far as he knows, Eric remains in prison. He is most likely suffering, and his life could end at any moment. Since Elizabeth's demise always ended violently, there could be no more appropriate setting than a prison to facilitate Eric's murder. Perhaps his incarceration is a result of the curse as well.

Eric's impending danger and long absence tugs at Eli's heart. If only he could turn back time and prevent Castor from derailing the sobriety program. He would still have his sober companion with him and everything would be as it should. Instead, he is condemned to rot of the Dry Death for an unknowable length of time. Eric could die while Castor has him hostage. Perhaps that is Castor's intention? To punish Eli for being a bad son by keeping him from the one person in his life that means the most to him?

Eli considers Cicero's advice to accept his soul mate as-is and turn him into a vampire, despite meaning he would never have the physical relationship with Elizabeth that he is accustomed to. Can he live with that? Does it even matter? Does a soul mate have to be a physical mate, or is love of this magnitude strong enough to transcend the boundaries of a typical relationship? What would it mean to have Eric as his lifelong soul mate? Would they be more than friends? Would their pairing create something completely new? A new way for two beings to love each other not based on traditional gender roles?

With nothing but time and agonizing hunger to keep him company, Eli fights to avoid falling into complete madness by searching his soul for what he truly wants. During one particularly vivid hallucination, he laughs when he sees Castor and the vampires manifest in his room.

"You do not belong in my mind," Eli mumbles with a laugh. "I can control who I let in my mind."

"We are not in your mind, Elias," Castor says.

A vampire unlocks the chains around Eli's hands and steps away.

Eli rubs the ruts in his wrists and squints at Castor, hoping if he blinks enough Castor and the others will disappear and he can return to more pleasing hallucinations.

But Castor remains. He signals to vampires outside the room to bring someone into Eli's room. Immediately, Eli detects the heavy scent of fresh human blood and his hunger ignites. He watches in horror as the vampires drag a bloodied and beaten Eric into his room. Eric's face has cuts and bruises from where Jeremiah happily brutalized him, or as he calls it, tenderized him. Blood drips from the corner of Eric's mouth, his lip busted and his gums bleeding after Jeremiah's pounding.

Eli and Eric are equally shocked to see each other. Finally, they both understand the motive behind their captivity. Castor plans to force Eli into killing Eric.

Chapter Thirteen

Castor's vampire bouncers carelessly toss Eric onto the floor of Eli's holding room. They throw him hard enough to send him somersaulting into the cement wall. The vampires laugh and pull the door closed, and Castor remains outside the locked door to taunt Eli from the safety of the hallway.

"I took the liberty of ending both the Dry Death and your sobriety for you, Elias," Castor says. "It pains me to see you in such agony."

Eli's hunger rages as the smell of Eric's blood floods his nose. "Get him out of here, Castor!" He curses.

"Oh, and your indiscretion will be videotaped, I'm afraid," Castor says, feigning an empathetic tone. "Vampires and humans alike will see your fall from grace as evidence the great Elias Alexander is a hypocrite and a villain. They will see the blood rehabilitation program does not work, and that Salvation is no salvation at all. They will call for change, for a new beginning. And I will be there to hold the collective hand of the country. I will lead them in a new direction, towards life as it should be. With vampires as the dominant species."

Eric groans and rolls onto his back. Eli watches him like a starving lion stalks its prey in the wilderness.

"Elias, my son. One day, you will see the error of the human way, and you will stand with your father once again."

"Castor. Father, I am begging you. If you ever loved me at all, please … take him out of here," Eli pleads. He plasters himself against the wall, the point farthest away from Eric. "Please do not make me do this!"

"There's that word again, Elias. *Love*. Do you see now? It does you no good. Had you been loyal to me, we wouldn't be here. Your little pet would be free to live his life, at least for a little while longer."

Eric coughs and swallows the blood in his mouth. Aware of Eli's severe state of starvation, he knows Eli won't be able to hold out for long.

"You're a coward!" Eric yells. "You give vampires a bad name. Eli is a good man, a better man than you could ever dream of being. I hope I live to see the day he takes you down!"

Castor chuckles. "Young Eric. You will not live to see another minute."

Boisterous laughter echoes through the stone hallway as Castor and his vampires trail away, leaving Eli to tear Eric apart.

Eli turns and plants his face against the cold stone wall, his body burning with starvation.

Eric stands. "Eli, can you open this door? Can you get us out of here?"

"No," Eli grunts. Every ounce of his energy evaporates into his efforts to keep himself from attacking Eric. "I am not strong enough."

"But you could if you feed, right?"

"They don't exactly have synthetic blood room service here, Eric," Eli says, managing a small laugh. He grunts and groans, his strength flailing as he exhausts his efforts to restrain his inner animal.

"Feed," Eric says, his voice now too close.

Eli spins around to see Eric standing directly in front of him.

"It's our only chance of getting out of here!"

"No!" Eli growls, stumbling to the opposite side of the room in a futile effort to avoid him.

Eric pursues him. "Elias, if you don't get us out of here, they will kill us!"

"*I might kill you*," Eli growls. "Get away from me! Please!"

"You won't kill me. You know how to control it. *Feed*," he says. He brings his wrist up to Eli's mouth.

"No! Eric, I don't want to hurt you!"

"You're our only chance!" Eric yells. Hoping an abrupt act of violence will push him over the edge, he hauls off and slugs Eli in the jaw.

It does precisely what he expects.

Eli growls, fangs bared, and grabs Eric's arm. He plunges his fangs into the veins and starts drinking vigorously.

Eric feels both relief and terror. Knowing this is the only chance either of them has at escaping Castor's custody alive, he wants Eli to drink as much blood as he needs to regain his strength. But the threat looms that Eli could lose total control and kill him. The pain of inch-long fangs inside his wrist tearing veins and flesh is excruciating, and he clenches his teeth to keep himself from screaming.

Eli feels the delicious red nectar bringing his body back to life. The pain of the Dry Death is enough to send any creature into permanent madness, even one with as much self-control as he has. The quelling of his hunger is staggering, but it is the absorbing of Eric's emotions and his blood's memory that throws him into ecstasy.

Delivering a satisfying answer to the question that has been burning within him, the remnants of Elizabeth's emotions do indeed remain in Eric's blood and they flood into Eli's body and mind. If any doubt remained as to Eric's true identity, it now washes away as the blood stamped with Elizabeth's timeless memories soaks into Eli's body.

Eric's memories and emotions are powerfully intriguing and Eli ingests them gluttonously, hungry to see into his soul.

Eric is scared. He has been savagely beaten, starved, and terrorized.

But Eric is still hopeful.
Eric trusts him.
He believes in him.
And ...
Eric loves him.

Eli withdraws his fangs. His body requires more blood, but the verification that his soul mate of a thousand years stands before him compels him to momentarily stop feeding. He grabs the sides of Eric's face.

"It truly is you!"

"Eli, we have to get out of here! They plan to kill us." Eric says in a rushed voice.

He pulls at Eli's arms, unable to budge them. He suspects Eli is hallucinating from the Dry Death and that the sudden consumption of blood is causing him to lose control of his emotions as has previously happened.

"I have wanted to know for so long," Eli says. His eyes are a blur of tears and they stream freely down his pale cheeks.

"Eli, you need to focus."

"I don't know what we're going to do with you being a guy and all," Eli says with a bloody grin.

"What? Eli, try to focus!"

Eric is startled when Eli plants a bloody kiss right on his mouth, then hugs him fiercely.

"What are you doing?"

"I don't know! I'm just so happy it's really you!" Eli exclaims. His strength wanes and his knees buckle but he steadies himself. "I'm pretty sure this is the best day of my entire life!" he raves.

"You're not back to normal yet, are you?" Eric says.

"No," he says, panting. "I need more blood."

Eric pulls back from Eli's steel hug turns his head, exposing his neck. "Do it."

Eli sees the blood pulsing through the jugular under Eric's skin and his mouth waters.

"Are you sure?"

"Yes. Just try to hurry, Jeremiah and Castor are -"

Eric's train of thought is cut short as he feels the fangs puncture his neck. He gasps and a groan of pain escapes him.

"Oh God that hurts a lot more than I expected!" he says gritting his teeth.

Most vampires prefer the stronger blood flow from biting the neck over any other part of the human body, and Eli is no different. It works to replenish his body and bring back his vitality, which he hasn't had since before entering blood rehab months ago. If it were up to him, this moment would never end. He meets his hunger needs while reaching Eric on the most intimate level possible: that of his mind and emotions.

"Stop now ... Stop!" Eric says, growing weak.

Eli, punch-drunk on blood and emotion, can barely hear Eric's voice over the raging sound of blood coursing into his body.

"Eli! You have to stop. I think I'm ... I'm going to pass out," he says, his body losing strength from the blood drain.

From a reserve of strength he did not know exists within him, Eli rouses himself from the blood stupor and withdraws his fangs. On the brink of passing out, Eric starts to fall but Eli wraps his arms around him, clutching him tightly as one would a life vest, and eases him down to the floor. Eli rests over him, holding him in the protective bear hug while breathing raggedly and battling to regain his composure. Eric's heart beat is slow but steady, indicating Eli stopped feeding just in time.

Eric is vaguely aware that the feeding has stopped, and feels Eli's weight on him. His strength is sapped and he can only lay there, a weakened lamb in the lion's grip. His vision blurs and blackens, and an inconvenient wave of nausea flows through him. Eli hears the impending purge and rolls Eric onto his side just in time for him to vomit on the floor.

"Eric," Eli whispers. "It's okay. We are getting out of here."

Voices coming from down the hall grab Eli's attention and a

sinister smile spreads across lips still dripping with Eric's blood.

"Stay here. Rest. I'll be back."

The destruction Eli unleashes upon Castor's vampires is quick and merciless. Heads are ripped from shoulders and hearts are impaled reducing the vampire bodies to ash. Eli rips his way through twelve vampires, saving Jeremiah and Castor for last.

Castor retreats to the open meeting room and sits at the large table as he listens to Eli rip and rage through his men. Jeremiah stumbles into the room, appropriately frightened by a full strength Eli hot on his trail.

"Castor! Castor, protect me!" Jeremiah cries. He runs behind Castor and cowers behind him.

Eli follows close behind, stopping just short of the table. He feels more powerful than ever as Eric's blood courses through his veins.

"Feels good, does it not?" Castor says casually. "To feed again. Naturally, the way we were meant to."

"I can end you if I want, Father," Eli says.

"No you can't! He's an original, older and stronger than you! You don't stand a chance against him!" Jeremiah shrieks.

"I can definitely end *you*," Eli growls.

Castor holds up a hand. "Stop, Elias. There is no need to proceed. You have served your purpose. The video of your transgression is already on its way to the media. You may leave. Just dispose of young Eric's body."

Eli laughs. "I did not kill him as you wanted me to, Father."

Castor raises an eyebrow. "No?"

"No. Unlike you, I have respect for human life. I do not seek to submit another race for my own benefit."

"Yet you just murdered vampires without a second thought? You are a hypocrite, Elias. You shun your own kind for the benefit of the weaker race. You are a disgrace."

"A disgrace? You took my life by force! You chose this life for me, not I! And you would seek to destroy anyone with the courage to stand up to you, even your own son!"

"Just kill him already, Castor!" Jeremiah shouts. "What are you waiting for? We don't need him anymore!"

"Say another word, Jeremiah, and I will end you," Castor says coldly.

"Who did you send the video to?" Eli demands. "Tell me and I will spare both of your lives."

"You are in no position to threaten me, Son," Castor says.

"You mistakenly believe you are the only vampire with resources and connections, Father. I can have you arrested and put to death with one phone call. I have enough evidence to give the human authorities to justify such an action. Do not think I will not do it. Tell me who has the video!"

"I told you. It is too late. Your fate is sealed."

Eli rushes Jeremiah and tears him away from Castor's protective reach. He squeezes his head and prepares to twist.

"I will separate your head from your body if you do not tell me right now where the video was sent!"

"CNN!" Jeremiah whimpers. "It was sent to CNN!"

"Blast you, Jeremiah!" Castor hisses. He stands up and rushes Jeremiah, tearing him from Eli's grip. "Burn for your betrayal!" He snaps Jeremiahs neck and rips his head from his body.

Eli stumbles back and prepares to defend against Castor, but Castor does not attack. Instead, he grabs Eli's arms and steadies him.

"You cannot stop this, Son. My plans are in motion. This is much bigger than you. Humans will fall from power, and we will rise to see a new way of life."

"You are an endless disappointment," Eli says quietly. He pulls away from Castor's grip. "I will fight this to the bitter end. I will stop you."

"Then you will die, Elias. Defeated and alone."

"No, Father. I am not alone."

Eli intercepts the video of him feeding on Eric by calling in a favor to Ashley Taylor, the young reporter he met at the Maverick.

As far as he knows, the public will never see his transgression.

It is the next night before Eric awakens from coma-like sleep. Having lost so much blood and being starved by Castor's vampires has left him gaunt and weak. He opens his eyes and glances sleepily around, sighing with relief as he realizes he is in his old room at Eli's townhouse. The light in the room is off but the full moon in the clear night sky outside casts a soft blue glow allowing Eric to see Eli leaning in the doorway smiling softly.

"How long have I been out?" Eric asks. He sits up and leans back against the headboard.

"Over twenty four hours," Eli answers.

Eric gingerly presses his forehead and grimaces. "I feel like I got hit by a truck."

Eli chuckles and strides to the bed, sitting down on the edge. "That sounds about right. You've been through hell. Beaten, starved, and drained of nearly all your blood." Eli's voice is remorseful and he looks down at the floor.

"Hey," Eric says, his throat dry and voice crackling. "Don't sound so dejected about it. It got us free, didn't it?"

"It did," Eli says. "Thank you for allowing me to … feed from you."

"Eli, how could your father do this to you?"

"Father and I always had a complicated relationship," Eli answers.

"Complicated? So he always tries to kill you and the people you love?"

Eli glances at him. "It is not always this dramatic," he says. "Believe it or not, we have had periods where we got along very well. Just not recently. The rift in our difference of opinion has become a chasm. He crossed the line this time. "

"With the vampire espionage?"

"Yes. And, with you."

Eric considers him for a moment. He wants to know once

and for all, too.

"So did you learn anything? When you drank my blood, what did you see in the remnants?"

Eli shifts to face him. "I learned much," he says. "I feel a bit guilty when I consume a human's remnants."

"Why guilty?"

"It is an intimate intrusion. Reading the emotions and memories, seeing into a human's life without their permission."

"And? What did you see with me? Am I ... am I Elizabeth?"

"Yes, Eric. You are her reincarnation."

"Holy shit," Eric says with a heavy sigh. "This is unbelievable."

"Her reincarnation has never happened this way."

"You mean she's never come back as a guy, right?"

Eli laughs awkwardly. "Yes. This is a first."

"Do you know what made things different?"

"No," Eli says, rubbing his face. "Cicero and I have considered the issue tirelessly, but we do not understand it."

"Where is Cicero, anyway?"

"He is stuck somewhere between here and Scotland, having Visa problems. Another ploy by Castor to thwart my efforts."

"So if what you say is true, and if I'm really a reincarnated soul that is damned to die when I'm twenty five, then ... I have a birthday coming up, Eli. I won't be twenty five much longer."

"I know, Eric. I know."

"Is there any way to stop this?"

"For as long as the curse has been in effect, I have been researching methods to break it. There are none, save for asking Moriah to do it, but I do not think she would even if I could find her. No one has spoken her name for nearly as long as she cursed us."

"It doesn't make sense the curse would suddenly change like this. What if it means it's ending, and my lifetime is the last one? And if I die, that's it. No more Elizabeth, and no more *me*."

"To be honest, I worry about the same thing."

Eric throws up his hands. "Then we have to do it."

"Do what?"

"You have to turn me."

"Eric, this isn't something to rush into lightly."

"What's to think about? I don't want to die, Eli. My options aren't that great, but I'd rather continue to exist than ..."

Eric realizes the reason Eli isn't jumping at the chance to turn him.

"Oh, wow," he says sheepishly. "I am so blind. You can't turn me. You'd never get Elizabeth back if you do."

"Eric, I -"

"No, it's okay, really," Eric says. He tosses the covers off his legs and labors to maneuver himself to the edge of the bed. He pushes himself up and leans a hand on the nightstand to steady himself. "Wow, I am really weak."

"Let me help you," Eli says as he stands and grabs Eric's arm to support him.

"I'm fine, Eli. I don't need your help."

Eli lets go but follows behind him as he makes his way across the hall to the bathroom.

"You know I can't stay here, right?" Eric says. He braces himself against the doorway and tries to catch his breath.

"What do you mean?"

"I'm an escaped prison inmate, remember? They'll be looking for me."

"But I can protect you here," Eli says. "If you leave, your time may come and if I'm not there ..."

"Not there to watch me die?" Eric glances over his shoulder at him.

Eli curses under his breath. "That is not what I mean, Eric, I simply -"

"It's okay, Eli. I understand. But as soon as I can walk without passing out," he says as he slides down the wall unable to stand any longer. "As soon as ..."

"Eric!" Eli leans over him and lightly taps his cheek as his eyes close and his head falls forward. "Eric, wake up."

Eric's head bobs back up and he struggles to hold his eyes open.

"Here, let me help you get back to bed. You need to rest."

"Eli, listen," Eric says. He grabs Eli's arm. "You saved my life."

"I nearly killed you!" Eli says, pain crossing his features.

"So we have a difference of opinion," Eric mumbles. He laughs as his body betrays his efforts to move and relentless fatigue sets in. "Let me die. If it means you get your true love back, when the time comes, just let me die."

"Eric!"

"I would do that for you, Eli. Not for anyone else, and especially ... not a ... vampire ..."

Eli's efforts to wake him fail for Eric's exhaustion is too great. Eli picks him up and carries him to his room where he lays him on the bed and covers him up. He steps back and watches his sleeping companion take slow, shallow breaths. Then, he falls to his knees.

What Eli feels for Eric is completely new for him. It is raw and powerful, and a bit confusing. Knowing he has Elizabeth's soul brings him great joy, but still, he is not Elizabeth, at least physically. He can't deny his desire to hold her again as he always had. If he chooses to let Eric die, he could lose them both forever. But if he turns Eric, he will never have her back.

An instinct has been tugging at the corner of his mind for some time now, and Eli finally decides to heed it. His greatest conflict lies with his true desire to save Eric. He doesn't want to give up on seeing Elizabeth again, but what feels worse to him is the idea of losing Eric. For whatever reason, be it their easy friendship or the intense bond he feels with him since consuming his blood, Eli can't fathom letting Eric die. If asked to explain how he feels about Eric, he could not find the words to do so. The only thing he knows for sure, is that he loves him.

The next morning, Eli leaves a tray on the nightstand with breakfast and a note. Eric doesn't hear him leave, but when he awakens the first thing he does is read the note:

Gone to help Frank find new location for Salvation production. Stay inside. Keep door locked. I have my phone. Eat something because you are paler than I am.

Eric chuckles at Eli's dry attempt at humor. But he has no intention of eating, or of staying inside. Instead, he drags himself out of bed and gets dressed, taking frequent breaks to catch his breath. The amount of energy required to do simple things saps his strength and he continues to glance at his watch in fear that he's moving too slow to leave before Eli gets back.

Finally at the front door ready to leave, he wraps his coat around him and glances out the window down the streets to be sure no National Guard or police are nearby. He lays his cell phone and the note for Eli on the small table by the coat rack. He figures this way, Eli won't be able to call or text him and influence the decision he is about to make. It's better for Eli this way. At least he'll be safe.

Eric heads out into the chilly morning, pulling his hood up over his head and keeping his head down as he makes his way to perdition.

Eli senses something is wrong after getting no response from several text messages to Eric. Flanked by their police escort, Eli and Frank successfully locate a permanent facility ideal to the mass production of Salvation and they set their attorneys to writing up the paperwork that would allow them to begin production.

Eli leaves Frank to continue the meetings and heads back home, his pace quickened by the dread filling his heart. It is dark when he returns home, but he immediately senses Eric's absence.

"Eric?" He calls out despite being certain there will be no answer. He sees the note on the table and tosses his house keys down as he picks it up. "No," he breathes. "Damn it, why?" He reaches for his phone but realizes trying to call Eric would be pointless, given his cell phone rests on the table. "What have you done?" He shouts, violently turning the table over sending it flying across the room. He rereads the note.

I am your friend. But a fugitive, I am not. I owe 2 years on my sentence. Since I won't live that long, just know that I believe in you. And, I hope you find her again. -E

Eli scrambles to think of what to do. An idea immediately comes to him and he grabs Eric's cell phone from across the room where it landed along with the table. He searches for the contact, and sure enough, it's still there.

"Thank God," Eli says. He calls the number, and to his relief, she answers.

"Hello?"

"Robin, this is Elias Alexander. I need your help."

Chapter Fourteen

"Robin? What's the verdict?" Eli sits at the table and mouths to Cicero that it's about Eric as he holds the phone tightly to his ear anticipating the news. It has been a month since Eric turned himself in, but the altered state of affairs in society rendered it nearly impossible to find out his status, until now.

"Eric is still at the county jail. With things being so harried and martial law still in effect, the normal legal processes are sort of at a standstill."

"That's good, right? I mean, jail is better than prison, right?"

"Well, that depends," she says with some concern. "In prison he would likely be in his own cell, but with the county jail being so full it's probably not very comfortable for him."

Eli sighs. "Okay, what can we do to get him out? If everything is on such a legal hiatus, can't we get him out on some temporary release? What about another work assignment?"

"I think you know the sober companion program is frozen indefinitely," she says.

"For now, yes, but maybe he can serve in a similar capacity that the court would approve of. Maybe something to do with the distribution of Salvation?"

Robin grumbles in frustration. "It's a long shot, Elias," she says. "I can try to file with the appeals court tomorrow morning. There's no guarantee they'll see his case right away though."

"Do what you can, Robin. Let me know when you hear

anything."

"I will."

"And, Robin? Thank you for what you're doing for him," Eli says quietly. "He doesn't deserve any of this."

Robin is silent for a moment before clearing her throat. "Eric is one of a kind, Elias. He's lucky to have a friend like you."

A friend, he thinks to himself. *Do others feel despondent and heartbroken when a mere friend is just beyond reach?* "Thank you, Robin," he says.

Cicero holds out his hands and raises his eyebrows. "Well? Are we gettin' him out?"

"She is filing an appeal. But there's no way to tell if we'll get this done in time." Eli leans back and crosses his arms over his chest. "I do not know what to do, Cicero."

"Aye," Cicero says.

"I should not have left him alone that day," Eli says. "Then he would not have gone and done this. It is my fault he is incarcerated."

"It's nae yer fault, Eli. Eric is an honorable man. He turned himself in because it was his moral and legal obligation. Ye wouldn't have been able to stop him."

"Perhaps not. But still. I cannot help but feel responsible."

A knock at the door startles them both.

"Who could that be at this hour?" Cicero groans.

Eli jumps up. "Despite your tendency to be a grump, I am glad you are back, Cicero," Eli says with a wink.

"Bah," Cicero mutters. "Get the door already."

Eli silently chides himself for feeling a sudden rush of hope that the guest at the door could be Eric. His heart's desire grows stronger every day.

He pulls open the door.

"Elizabeth?"

How can this be? Standing before him, in original form, is his Elizabeth. She is as striking as ever, classily dressed as sophisticated, a modern day beauty.

"Hello, Elias," she says. The sound of her soft voice and the sight of her familiar smile and sparkling blue eyes nearly bring him to his knees.

"Elizabeth? How is this possible? Wait! Do you *know* me?"

She nods. "Yes, Elias. I remember everything!"

Stunned, Eli stares at her unable to speak.

She laughs gently. "I knew you would be in shock. May I come in?"

He swings the door wide for her and engulfs her in a firm hug. "My God," he breathes. "My God."

"I know, my love. I know it is difficult to believe, but it is me! I have found you!"

Cicero walks out of the kitchen to see what is going on.

"Who is it?" He calls.

Eli releases the woman from his embrace and steps to the side so Cicero can see her.

As soon as their eyes meet, Cicero is overcome by a feeling of dread. He stares at the woman, immediately sensing a sickening hollowness about her. He looks at Eli, whose animated expression indicates he is oblivious to the creature standing next to him.

"Cicero! It's Elizabeth! It's actually her!" Eli studies her face in amazement.

Elizabeth blushes and nods politely. "Hello, Cicero," she says.

Cicero does not return the greeting, but instead looks at Eli like he's a madman.

On some level, Eli is disturbed by Cicero's detached response, but the shock of seeing Elizabeth's face entangles his thoughts and senses. He hugs her again, both of them laughing like happy children.

"How is this possible?" Eli says, holding her face in his hands. "How can you be here and know who I am?"

"We have much to talk about, Elias!"

They both glance at Cicero whose stone expression makes

them jointly uncomfortable.

"Please, come into the sitting room. It is warm by the fire," Eli says, leading her by the hand.

She happily takes his hand and follows him, glancing over her shoulder at Cicero as she does.

"Cicero, break out the wine! This is unbelievable!" Eli calls.

Eli and Elizabeth sit together on the love seat by the fire, holding each other and gazing into each other's eyes.

"Is this even real?" Eli says, his voice as high as his spirits.

"Yes! Yes, Elias it is real!"

"But how? Where have you been? It's been over fifty years!"

"I do not have all the answers, Elias, but I just celebrated my twenty fifth birthday. When I woke up on that day, I remembered everything! You, the past millennium, the witch's curse. All of it!"

"This is incredible!" Eli gushes.

"I am not certain, but I believe the curse to be broken!"

"Why do ye say that?" Cicero says quietly. He sets the wine and glasses on the small end table and pours.

She looks at him briefly, her smile fading as she does, but then turns her attention back to Eli.

"It's just a feeling. I have never remembered everything before. Well, without being close to death. I have this amazing feeling that it's over!"

"My God! We have to celebrate. We'll go out, the three of us! Just let me check my phone. Someone has been calling it non-stop!" He jumps up and jogs to the kitchen for his cell phone.

Cicero smiles smugly at the intruder and follows Eli.

"What the hell are ye doin'?" he whispers.

Eli picks up his phone from the table but is too late to catch the call.

"Wow, I wonder what they want," he says.

"Who?" Cicero asks.

"Oh, the kids at the magic shop down the street. I have 5 missed calls from them." A text message pops up on his screen and he opens it.

Nathan and Diane: "We made some progress! Stone dagger doesn't kill witches, thank goodness. But it turns them into stone. Still researching curses. Talk to you soon!"

Eli shrugs. "Nothing major," he says and lays the phone back down.

"Didn't ye hear me?" Cicero prods, growing impatient.

"What, Cicero? What did you say?"

Annoyed by Eli's sudden display of giddiness, Cicero tries to temper his words to avoid setting him off. "There are a couple of things wrong here. First," he whispers fiercely and glances around to be sure the imposter woman can't hear him, "*first,* who the hell is that? 'Cause it's nae Elizabeth!"

"What are you talking about? Of course it is. She looks the same as before!"

"I don't know what that thing is, but it's nae her. And secondly, Elias, where in the bloody hell is your head? Have ye already forgotten about Eric?"

"Eric," Eli says. His thoughts are foggy and all he feels is an inflated sense of elation about seeing Elizabeth. "Eric is …"

"*In jail! Still alive!* If he's still alive," he juts a finger out and points in the woman's direction, "then who in the devil is *she?*"

"I don't know how, Cicero, but if the curse is broken then maybe they're both alive?"

"Ach!" Cicero curses loudly, glancing around nervously. "All right. Just tell me one thing. Can ye smell her blood? 'Cause I cannot. Is she even human?"

Eli thinks about it and blinks away the doubt creeping into his mind. "No, but that doesn't mean anything. Many humans take the chemicals -"

"There are no chemicals anymore, remember? Have you completely lost yer mind Elias?"

"Whatever, you're just jealous," Eli barks.

"What? Jealous? Do you even hear yourself? What's wrong

with ye? What about Eric?"

Up close, Cicero just now notices a thin milky film over Eli's normally deep, dark eyes.

"Wait a minute," he says suspiciously. He leans in close to get a better look. "What the devil is wrong with yer eyes?"

"Cicero, you are starting to anger me," Eli says, his voice oddly flat.

Cicero squints. "Yer eyes, they're foggy. Somethin's wrong with ye, and I'll bet it has to do with whoever that woman is!"

"You mind your manners!" Eli snaps.

Taken aback by Eli's sudden aggression, Cicero throws his hands up and backs away.

Eli rejoins Elizabeth in the sitting room, hugging her again. She covers his face in kisses and they laugh like two teenagers in love.

Cicero peers out from the kitchen watching them, suspicion marinating in his bones. A clever idea sneaks into his mind and he sneaks a look at Eli's phone. With Eli distracted, Cicero picks up his cell phone to read the text from the magic shop.

"Cicero!"

Eli's boisterous voice startles him. He spins around and feels the urge to heave as Eli and the woman enter the kitchen with arms around each other.

"Let's go out and celebrate!"

"Ye know we can't do that, Elias," Cicero says fishing for an excuse. "Have ye forgotten there's still a curfew for us?"

"Uh, hello Cicero, my name is Elias Alexander, and I can go wherever I want because I'm saving us from another war!"

Cicero scowls at the sarcasm.

"Elias, you must tell me how you knew to use Salvation to replace the synthetic blood!" Elizabeth gushes.

"I want to tell you everything," Eli says.

"Why don't we just stay here then," Elizabeth insists. "Please. We have so much to talk about." She looks pointedly at Cicero.

"For God's sake, Cicero," Eli growls. "If you cannot manage

to be civil, then you can leave. Allow me to reunite with Elizabeth in peace!"

"Fine," Cicero snaps. "By all means, reunite with whoever that thing is!"

"Cicero!" Eli shouts.

"Calm down, my love," Elizabeth says. "He is merely confused." She glares at the fiery Scottish vampire.

Cicero points at Eli. "This is wrong, Elias. *Dead wrong.*" He storms out of the townhouse and slams the door closed behind him.

Eli and Elizabeth sigh together. "I am so sorry about him," Eli says, brushing a hair from her face. "You know Cicero. He can be difficult at times."

"It is no matter to us now," Elizabeth says.

"I still cannot believe it is you! Tell me, how did you find me? What have you been doing in this lifetime?"

"My story isn't special, Eli," she says bashfully.

"But I want to know everything!"

"We have all the time in the world for that. But I am dying to know how you saved us from a War with Salvation!"

Eli blinks. "Oh, well, it is no big secret, Elizabeth. My friend was able to replicate the formula and we have been working to manufacture it. Must we talk about such things right now?" He pulls her close to him. "Can we not talk about more pleasant things?"

"Do you know the formula? It is being kept from the public. I am just so curious."

"The right people know the formula, the ones willing to use it to benefit our kind."

"I asked you for the formula," she says, her voice growing cold and strong.

The room begins to darken supernaturally. A current of cold air from an unknown source swirls around them and the walls begin to creak and moan as if something were squeezing them. Eli looks around, puzzled.

"What is happening?"

Elizabeth rolls her eyes. "Honestly, I couldn't care less about Salvation," she says.

Eli feels an invisible force push against his abdomen. He looks down and sees nothing, but the force strengthens enough to pull him off of the loveseat and throws him against the wall of the sitting room where he is held suspended against it, unable to move.

"What is this?" The cloudiness over his eyes disappears and he sees the woman's true form. He gasps. "Moriah!"

"Now you're making sense," she says coldly. She stands up and begins to walk in circles around the sitting room. "Castor wanted me to pry the Salvation formula out of you." She shrugs. "But I'd rather talk to you about something else."

"You evil creature! How could you have done this to me? All these years, forcing Elizabeth to die over and over! No devil could be as cruel as you!"

Moriah throws her head back and laughs. "You know what's really amusing about this, Eli? For a thousand years, you think this was all about you!"

"What do you speak of, witch?" Eli shouts. He struggles against the force pinning him against the wall but still cannot move.

"Here, darling," she says in a patronizingly sweet voice. "Let me show you." She walks to him and touches his leg, instantly forcing his mind into a flashback.

It is the night of the curse. He sees himself, and Elizabeth, through someone else's eyes. The watcher follows them out of Elizabeth's large estate home as they run under moonlight into the dark forest. There is a fire in a grassless patch of forest waiting for them, one that Eli has just lit. As they reach their lover's nest, the watcher ducks behind a tree after a branch loudly snaps under her feet.

Elizabeth peers into the darkness. "Did you hear that?" she whispers.

"It is nothing," Eli says. He grabs her around the waste and pulls her close to him. "I am so happy to be with you this night, my love," he says.

"And I you," she responds.

Eli fights the flashback and pushes it from his mind. "Why are you showing me this, Moriah? Have you not made me suffer enough since that night?"

Her face darkens and she leers at him. "You did not see that night through *my* eyes!" She hisses. This time she grabs his leg and digs her fingernails into it. "*See!*"

The watcher sinks to her knees behind the tree as she watches the two lovers kiss passionately. But there is one detail Eli just now notices. The watcher's gaze is set on Elizabeth, not on Eli. He feels the watcher's angst as she watches Elizabeth canoodle with someone else. Someone that is not her.

Enraged and heartbroken, the watcher steps out from behind the tree, startling the two lovers.

"Moriah!" Elizabeth exclaims.

"Moriah!" Eli repeats. He steps away from Elizabeth. "What are you doing here? I thought your family had retired for the evening."

Moriah raises a finger, pointing at Elizabeth. "You," whispers.

Eli steps towards her. "Moriah, please listen," he begins to plead. "We did not intend for you to see us together. We did not intend to hurt you!"

"Moriah, I am sorry," Elizabeth says.

"You are a harlot!" she yells at Elizabeth.

"Moriah! Do not be cruel!" Eli belts.

Moriah begins to cry as she admires the beauty of Elizabeth's face as the soft oranges of the fire enhance her natural beauty. She grabs Elizabeth by the shoulders.

"How could you do this to me?"

"Moriah," Elizabeth says softly. "Please. I am sorry."

"How could you do this to me?" she shouts. She begins to ramble in a language neither of them can understand. A strong wind accosts the forest, blowing leaves from trees and violently whipping the flames of the fire.

"Elias!" Elizabeth calls out, afraid.

Eli comes to her side but stops short as he sees three men emerge from the shadows on the forest.

"Who are you?" he calls out. "Make yourself known!"

"They are your executioners, Elias," Moriah shrieks. She shakes Elizabeth hard. "And I am yours."

Elizabeth screams and struggles to tear herself away from Moriah's grip. She looks down at her left shoulder and her eyes widen as she sees smoke coming from beneath Moriah's palm. She cries out as the excruciating pain of the burned-in mark seethes on her skin. Moriah releases her.

"Do you see this, Elizabeth?" She screams, jerking Elizabeth's marked arm. "This mark means you are under my spell for all of eternity. No demon, no devil, and no witch can ever break this curse. You are forever damned, Elizabeth."

The three men restrain Eli and he finds them to be of incredible strength as he fights against them.

"And you!" Moriah screams. "You will walk this earth for all eternity and suffer the heartache that is mine this night. Turn him, Castor!"

"Elias!" Elizabeth screams.

"Elizabeth!" Eli wrenches away from his attackers. The man Moriah calls Castor grabs him by the neck. To Eli's absolute horror, he sees fangs slide out in the man's mouth. "Monster!" Eli screams. "Monster!"

Castor plunges his fangs into Eli's neck and drains him. Moriah watches at first, then turns her attention back to Elizabeth.

"I loved you," Moriah cries. "I loved you and you betrayed me!"

"No," Elizabeth says, eyes blurred with tears.

"Die!" Moriah screams. She plunges a knife into Elizabeth's stomach.

"NO! Elizabeth!" Eli manages to scream as his body weakens from the blood drain.

Elizabeth falls to her knees, holding her stomach. Blood gushes over her hands and her body begins to die.

"You will die. Over and over again, Elizabeth," Moriah says. She falls to her knees in front of her dying love. "All I ever did was love you," she says, voice softening. "And now, all you will ever do ... is die."

Moriah takes her hand off Eli. He stares down at her in horror.

"My God," he breathes, the flashback of Moriah's emotions forcing tears out of him. "All this time, I thought I broke your heart. We were betrothed to be married, our parents wanted us paired. I thought this was all my fault."

"It is equally your fault, Elias," she says. "I didn't love you. I loved her. And *you* took her away from me."

Eli hangs his head. "I am sorry for the pain we caused you," he says. "But how do you justify this with a millennium of torture? Will you not end this curse once and for all? Have you not punished us enough?"

Eli raises his head when he hears the knock at the door.

Moriah tilts her head. "Who could that be, Elias?" She says, her voice dripping in sarcasm.

"I do not know," Eli says. "I was not expecting anyone."

"Oh, but I was," Moriah says. She winks at him and strides to the front door. Eli hears her greet the visitor. "Hello, darling."

"Is Eli here?"

Eli's heart sinks into his stomach as he hears Eric's voice.

"Yes, darling, he is waiting for you." Moriah lets Eric in and locks the door behind them.

"Eric! Eric, get out of here!" Eli shouts.

Hearing Eli's voice, Eric walks through the foyer and into the sitting room. He is taken aback as he sees Eli plastered to the wall and suspended off the floor.

"What the hell?" The birthmark on his arm suddenly singes under his shirt and he screams, ripping his coat off to get to the source of the pain. He smells the burning of his own flesh and claws at his arm, desperate for the pain to stop.

Moriah grabs him by the throat, picking him up inches off the floor and slamming him into the wall.

"Who are you?" He chokes.

"You know who I am. Eric. *Elizabeth.* Whoever you are," she says, bellowing a demonic laugh. "My, you are a cute one." She turns her head to glare at Eli. "No wonder you like this one so much." She turns back to Eric and kisses him hard, biting his lip at the end.

"Eli!" Eric shouts. "What's going on?"

"How did you get here, Eric?" Eli demands.

"They said someone negotiated my release," he says, grabbing at Moriah's hand around his neck. "It wasn't you?"

"I have been trying, Eric. All of us! But no, it was not me."

"It was me, you idiots," Moriah gloats.

"Moriah, please do not hurt him," Eli says. "I am begging you."

"I am begging you," she mimics. She snorts. "Please. After all these years, you are still such a passive man, aren't you?"

"What do you want, Moriah?" Eric says, his voice cracking as he tries to evade her chokehold.

"What do I want? Well, Elizabeth. Eric, whatever. After all these years, I got bored with the way things kept repeating, over and over, with no change. I wanted to mix things up a bit this time. See how you like falling in love with a boy," she says slyly glancing over her shoulder at Eli.

"What will it take for you to end this curse, Moriah?" Eli demands. "Please. I will do anything. Just spare his life."

Moriah laughs. "Spare his life? Oh, sweetheart. There's only one thing that can keep him alive, and you know what it is."

"That is it then? You are not willing to break the curse?"

"There is no breaking this curse, Elias." She glares at Eric. "When I set out to punish Elizabeth eternally for what she did to me, I meant it."

Eli sees something shiny in In Moriah's free hand. It comes into view. It is a long silver dagger with a jagged pattern, akin to a large hunting knife.

"Allow me this time, Elias, to be the one to murder your lover. Good bye, *Elizabeth*!" She hisses.

Moriah plunges the dagger into Eric's stomach and wrenches it up, the blade easily slicing through his flesh into his internal organs. Eric's scream hurts his own ears and the pain is unlike anything he ever felt. Shock sets in immediately and he feels his body giving in to the mortal wound. Moriah throws him onto the floor and laughs maniacally as she watches him writhe in pain.

"Eric! No!" Eli erupts in bloodcurdling screams as he watches Eric slump to the floor, smelling the rush of blood pouring out of him.

Moriah drops the knife and steps back, clapping her hands as she watches the reincarnation of her once deceitful lover die once again.

"Damn you to hell for this!" Eli cries.

"Hell?" She snorts. "Hell is for cowards, Elias. You and I will forever roam the hell that is on earth. Neither of us will ever have the love we so desire."

The front door crashes open and a gust of wind follows Cicero as he races in, a stone object in his hand.

"Your reign of terror is over, bitch!" Cicero yells. Before Moriah reacts, he rushes her and plunges the stone dagger into her heart. A bloodcurdling scream escapes her lips, and her face whitens as her body rapidly begins converting to stone. She bares her teeth and the final words of her life escape her mouth. "This isn't over!"

Moriah's stonification stops her powers and Eli falls hard onto the floor.

Stunned by the scene, Eli and Cicero stare at each other wide-eyed.

Eric groans loudly and falls onto his side.

"Eric!" Eli speeds to his side and nearly slips in the large pool of blood beneath him. He kneels beside him and turns him onto his back, supporting his head with his hand. "Don't try to talk. Just be still," Eli says. He looks up at Cicero. "Cicero, help me!"

Cicero shakes his head. "He's dying, Elias," he says grimly.

Cold tears drip from Eli's eyes and he clutches at Eric as he would his own life.

"Eric! I am so sorry I couldn't stop her from doing this," he stammers.

"You were under a spell," Cicero says.

"Eli," Eric says, his voice weak. He reaches a bloody hand up to Eli's face. "Eli, I can remember!"

Eli remains bent over and crying, his hunger unaffected by the fresh blood pooling around them.

"My god. I remember you! I remember everything," Eric says, smiling fondly as Elizabeth's memories flood his mind. "You loved her so much. So much …"

Eli's tears drip onto Eric's face and roll down his cheek. "Eric!"

"The curse, Eli," Eric says. "If you want to see Elizabeth again, you have to let me die."

Eli fervently shakes his head. "I will not lose you, Eric! I will not!"

"It's the only way …for you to see her … I know that's what you want." Eric's breathing becomes shallow as Death begins to take him.

"It is not her I want, Eric. I cannot begin to explain how I feel, but you are my soul mate and I do not want to be in this life without you. Stay with me. I will turn you but you must be the one to choose it." Seeing Eric's eyes begin to close, he shakes him gently. "Eric. You are my best friend. My best everything, and I truly love you."

"Eli," Eric murmurs, his body growing cold and numb as the life is nearly finished bleeding out of him. "When we first met … I really tried to hate you …but I couldn't, because it just seemed like we were supposed to be together."

Sobs escape Eli in spite of his efforts to control them.

Eric manages a weak smile. "I think I loved you from the very beginning. Now …you jerk … hurry up …and turn me."

"Do it now, lad!" Cicero prompts.

Eli wastes no time and sinks his fangs into Eric's throat. He drains what is left of Eric's blood, listening carefully as his heart slows and stops. The sheer elation of knowing Eric will be with him for all time mixes with the amorous emotions soaking into him through Eric's blood, producing a singular moment of ecstasy he will never forget. With the heart stopped, Eli bites his own wrist until it bleeds freely, then places it over Eric's mouth. The vampire blood soaks into the body and the reanimation process begins.

The turn is successful. Eric dies in his twenty fifth year of life and is reborn an immortal.

Chapter Fifteen

The Next Fall

The television runs at low volume in the background as Eli and Eric ready themselves in the dressing room. Streaming live in Manhattan, CNN's Ashley Taylor reports on the results of the groundbreaking election.

"In this monumental event, Elias Alexander wins the Senatorial vote for the State of New York. Winning in a landslide against human incumbent Senator McMann, Mr. Alexander also managed to outrun the oldest living vampire known as Castor earlier this year. Castor withdrew his bid from the Senate race after polls showed heavy favor towards Mr. Alexander and his platform of peace and equality. In this unprecedented age where vampires have won the right to vote and run for political office, there's no telling how far and how fast vampire equality will spread."

Eric glances at the television, then at Eli.

"You realize Castor is going to retaliate against you for this, right?"

"Of that I am certain. But I will deal with it when it

happens."

"You ready for this?" Eric asks jovially.

"Ready as I'll ever be," Eli says. He scrutinizes his reflection in the mirror and nods in approval.

Eric snorts. "Seriously? How do you not see this is crooked?" He steps in front of Eli and straightens the red silk tie.

"It looks fine to me," Eli says with a laugh.

"There. Now you're decent."

Eric straightens his own tie and they both double check their attire in the mirror. If looks could kill, the handsome duo could wipe out the country. Both wear navy blue suits with white undershirts, shiny black shoes, and devilishly styled hair.

"Do you think I should have gone with stripes?" Eli says nervously.

"The red tie is fine! Besides, you can't wear stripes if I'm wearing stripes."

"So you own the patent on stripes now?"

"No, I don't own the patent on stripes. What kind of question is that?"

"I don't know. It sounds like you think you own the patent on stripes." Eli smiles smugly.

"I hope this doesn't take too long. Captain Meyers is burning up my phone. Doesn't he realized we're at your acceptance speech?" Eric says.

"I am sure he is aware. I must admit, I very much look forward to sleuthing for the NYPD. Solving crimes is a rewarding endeavor."

"It's freaking awesome! I can't wait."

"You should have no problem with the blood remnant testing. You are lucky to have the blood of Elias Alexander running through your veins."

"Yes, the very *modest* blood," Eric mocks him with a smirk.

Eli grins.

"How are we going to find the time to solve crimes and be a

lawyer and a politician?"

"Oh, come on now," Eli chastises. "We do not sleep, remember? We have plenty of time to work in both capacities."

Eric turns away from the mirror to face him. "Hey, can I ask you something?"

"Of course." Eli continues to fiddle with his tie, causing it to go crooked again.

"Do you ever regret it?"

"Regret what?"

Eric leans in, voice lowered. "The choice you made … to keep me around, instead of her?"

Eli doesn't have time to answer as a woman raps quickly on the dressing room door and opens it. "It's time, gentlemen," she says, fidgeting with her microphone ear piece. "Follow me please."

Eli and Eric exchange confident smiles.

"Let's roll!" Eli says.

Followed by an entourage of associates and bodyguards, which includes Cicero and Dorothy, Frank Green, and Robin and her lawyer husband, Eli and Eric follow the woman through empty hallways and up a ramp where the roar of the crowd amplifies exponentially when they break through the felt curtain and proceed down the aisle towards the stage.

Humans and vampires of all ages and stations applaud fiercely and whistle, whoop, and holler their support of the New York State Senator. Eli stops to shake as many hands as possible, bodyguards restraining patrons as they thrust paper and pens at him hoping to get an autograph from the celebrity. The crowd roars in waves of approval as Eli stops to sign as many autographs as the guards will allow him. The oversized television monitors inside the stadium broadcast the live news coverage of the monumental event.

Finally, the entourage makes its way to the grandly decorated stage and gather around the podium, which Eli steps up to.

He waves and smiles, nodding politely at the fanatical crowd that overfills the indoor stadium. Red, white, and blue balloons, banners, glimmering posters, and signs decorate the already vibrant, colorful crowd. Waiting patiently for the applause to die down, Eli smiles brightly and prepares to give his speech.

"Ladies and gentlemen. Humans, vampires, and anything else out there," he says with a chuckle, his remark drawing fond laughter from the crowd. "I am humbled to stand here before you as the newly elected Senator for the great state of New York."

Another roar of whooping and applause rolls through the stadium.

"Thank you. I am honored that you chose me to represent the entire population of New York. And I will do just that: I will stand to give equal representation to every human and every vampire regardless of age, skin color, religion, political preference, sexual preference, and meal preference."

Another wave of laughter floats through the crowd. From behind him, Eric and Cicero exchange an ornery glance and smile at each other.

"The time of strife between humans and vampires is over. I declare this with no uncertainty. From this day forward, we will coexist peacefully. No race will ever again impose suppression or oppression upon the other. The fathers of this great country called for equality and freedom for all citizens, and we mean to enforce these ideals vigorously."

He smiles and again waits patiently as the crowd roars with approval.

"Make no mistake. We have a lot of work to do. But I am confident that by working in unison we will achieve our goals. No human will go without health insurance. No human will suffer discrimination for ethnic, political, economic, or racial status, nor sexual or religious preference. No vampire will suffer forced starvation, as freely donated human blood will be served in every restaurant, public attraction, and at established vampire feeding centers. And for those vampires that do not wish to consume live blood, the delicious drinks of the Salvation product line, created by my good friend Frank Green, will be as readily available in stores as a gallon of milk. Furthermore, vampires will now become a crucial part of the law enforcement process, as we use our telepathic abilities to help solve crimes and deter criminals from preying on the innocent."

Eli stops and lets the crowd roar wildly.

Eric nudges Cicero in the arm with his elbow. "The law enforcement was my idea," he says, winking.

"Yeah, whatever, ye cocky bastard!" he grumbles, but with a smile on his face.

"He really is going to change this world, isn't he?" Eric says.

Cicero snorts. "I've been sayin' it for a thousand years! Of course he is, he just couldn't focus on anything. Now that he's got ye to be at his side, he'll move mountains."

"Us," Eric says, nudging Cicero again. "He has us. We're family."

"Yeah, we're family. Now quit talkin' ye softie. Let the man finish his speech."

Eli continues. "In 1963, I was fortunate enough to witness a very important man give a very important speech. And his dream continues today. His American dream. The dream that at all men, all races, all creeds, are created equal. Created free. I want you to know that I will fight for your freedom. I will fight for equality! I will fight for the human race! I will fight for the vampire race! I will fight for all of us, so help me God! A new era begins, and it begins now!"

"Nice touch," Cicero says, pounding his hands together with the crowd as it explodes with energetic support.

Eli glances back at his entourage. "I want to thank all of you again for your support. And I want to thank my associates that stand behind me, both figuratively and literally here on the stage." He sweeps a hand behind him. "Let's hear it for them!"

The crowd loves the gesture and the applause grows louder.

Eli steps away from the podium and doles out hugs and handshakes to his team. When he gets to Cicero, he laughs.

"Cicero!" He gives him a hearty hug.

"Yeah, ye finally decided to listen to me!" Cicero says. "Proud of ye." He looks away to hide the prideful tears beginning to well in his eyes. "Move on, ye crazy bastard!"

Eli reaches Eric and embraces him tightly.

"Great speech!" Eric says. "Congratulations."

"None of this would have happened without you," Eli says. He pulls back and gazes into his best friend's eyes. "Thank you."

"Ah, come on. All I did was straighten your tie," Eric jokes, smiling warmly. His face turns serious, and he nods as he says, "You'll make one hell of a Senator, Elias."

"You'll make one hell of a legal advisor," Eli says with a wide smile.

Eric steps back to allow the Senator to continue thanking the rest of the group, but Eli catches his arm and pulls him in close. He speaks in a voice only Eric can hear.

"And no," Eli says.

"No, what?"

"No I don't regret choosing you over her. If I had to make the choice a thousand times, I'd make the same choice, a thousand and one times."

Eric drops his head and smiles.

"Eric. You're the best choice I've ever made. Don't ever forget that."

Eric raises his eyes to meet Eli's warm gaze. He grins and nods his head to the side. "The people await you," he says.

"Yes they do."

Just as Eli prepares to descend from the stage to meet and greet the voters, Captain Meyers bounds up the stairs followed by a police officer.

Noticing the harried expression on the Captain's normally stoic face, Eli greets him.

"Captain Meyers? Is something wrong?"

"You could say that, Alexander," the Captain says. He motions for Eli to come close and shows him a picture on his cell

179

phone. "Do you know what this is?"

Eli examines the picture of what appears to be a casually dressed man, but sees right away the dubious feature. The color drains from his face.

"His eyes," Eli says, voice falling into a whisper. "They are black?"

Captain Meyers nods. "Reports of these things are popping up all over the city, just within the last half hour. Some poor bastard managed to snap this picture before this thing attacked him in public view."

Eric and Cicero listen in while examining the eerie picture.

"What the devil?" Cicero mumbles.

"Eli, what is it?" Eric asks warily.

Eli's face darkens, the politician's smile sliding away.

"It is something I thought only to be a myth."

"A myth? What are we talking about here, Alexander?" Captain Meyers says in a rushed voice. "It's not a vampire?"

"That is no vampire, Captain," Eli says grimly.

"Well? What is it?" Eric asks.

Eli meets Eric's gaze and feels a tinge of regret for putting him in a suddenly perilous situation.

"That is a demon," Eli says. "And we are all in grave danger."

Continued in "The Manhattan Siege"
(SUMMER 2015)

About the Author

Emily Ford lives in the desert hotness of southern Arizona. She is the author of several series and standalone books in the thriller, horror, and paranormal genres. She is currently adapting novels into screenplays and has plans to move into film production in the near future. Inspired to reconnect with her creative side after thinking it was lost forever, Emily credits her sister, best-selling author Lizzy Ford, for being the reason she gave writing a chance, and is now planning a bright and exciting career in books and film.

Connect with Emily Ford

www.emilyfordworld.com
Twitter.com/EmilyFordWorld
Facebook.com/EmilyFordWorld
Pinterest.com/EmilyFordWorld

Other Books by Emily Ford

Crime Thriller Series
The Black Jester
The Silver Jester
The Blue Jester (2015)

Horror
Hell Town
The Demon Train
The Devil's Carnival

Paranormal
Supernatural Spies (2015)

www.ingramcontent.com/pod-product-compliance
Lightning Source LLC
Chambersburg PA
CBHW022112170626
46808CB00002B/705